No Place Like Home

A Patricia Fisher Cruise Mystery

Book 10

Steve Higgs

Dedication

To Jane Ballard who devised the outline of this story

and who has been a wonderful advocate.

Hi there,

Firstly, thank you for purchasing this book. I hope that you enjoy reading it anywhere near as much as I enjoyed writing it. Patricia Fisher is a character that came about quite by accident as you might have read in the dedication of the first book. I have come to love her quite dearly; she is so tenacious though she possesses almost no skills pertinent to the situations I put her in.

This is the final adventure for Patricia in her around the world odyssey. If you have not read the previous nine books, don't worry, each is a standalone story with a satisfying ending. However, they are chronological with her story developing as they continue. Patricia and her friends face danger and peril in each of them. Join her now as she comes to realise that there is **No Place Like Home** and look out for her continuing adventures as there are many new Patricia Fisher books to come even though this series has drawn to a close.

This is not my first series though; there are many other books already waiting for you. So, if you enjoy Patricia's adventures, you may wish to check out **Tempest Michaels**, **Amanda Harper** and **Jane Butterworth**. Like Patricia, they solve mysteries and their stories are written to make you laugh and keep you turning pages when you really ought to be going to sleep.

Finally, there is a secret **Patricia Fisher** story that is not available to buy anywhere. You can have *Killer Cocktail* for free though, just click the link below and tell me where to send it.

Yes! Send me my FREE Patricia Fisher story!

Table of Contents:

Trapped

An arm looped around my waist from behind and a hand clamped over my mouth. I tried to kick and scream and bite the hand, but he was far too strong and his hands far too big. He had his thumb looped over the bridge of my nose and two fingers under my chin, forcing my mouth shut as if he had been trained in how to kidnap a woman. A second man moved in to grab my legs, swiping my handbag as he did and patting me down to make sure I didn't have a phone tucked away anywhere.

Through panic-stricken eyes, I could see Mavis getting the same treatment a few yards ahead of me. The men carrying me followed her out of the house and down the steps where they split off to take me to the rear car as Mavis was taken to the one at the front.

This wasn't the plan!

I was supposed to stay in the house as they all left with Mathew. The next part of the plan was dangerous enough without me being in the boot of the car. What's more, no one knew I was here.

Still struggling as they carried me, I glimpsed the boot lid just before they swung me backward. That they were going to throw me in only occurred to me just as my body weight reached the apex of the backswing and started toward the car. They let go, allowing me to fly for a half second before I crashed into the unforgiving steel of the boot. If I didn't have enough bruises already, here were a few more to add to them.

The boot lid slammed down, shutting off all light and plunging me into darkness. It was a terrifying experience; yet another one to add to my list. Thunking sounds from the doors shutting and a settling of the suspension told me they were getting in the car. The engine started and the sensation of moving let me know we were on our way.

How on earth had I ended up in the boot of this car? It bumped out of the driveway and turned left along the road. I expected them to go right as that would be the swiftest route back to the motorway, so it was a good thing I had been prudent enough to ask that both eventualities be covered. The movement of the car was deeply unpleasant, rattling my insides which were already coiled upon themselves in fear. There wasn't so much as a blanket in the dark space to put under my head, not that it would have made a lot of difference to my comfort level if there had been: I was in so much discomfort from the trials of the last day. It seemed impossible that I had managed to fit so much into such a short space of time, yet here I was, bruised and battered from jumping out of a burning car, tattered and torn clothing to go with it, a bump to my head where I met the pavement to evade a car trying to run me over. Add to that the other failed attempts to kill me, all of which I had lived through by pure luck. Yet I couldn't feel sorry for myself because there were two other innocent people in the boots of the cars ahead of this one, and it was my fault they were going to die.

We had slim hope of getting out of this latest situation. Two chances out of three meant we were going to end up dead with only the nature of our demise yet to be decided.

I could hear voices talking inside the car, their words distorted and unrecognisable by the time they got through the seat fabric to my ears. Were they discussing me? Were they discussing what they were going to do with me and the other two when we arrived at the destination?

They were never going to get there, at least that was what I was telling myself. I had been cautious enough to enact a plan which would stop them, predicting their actions and their escape route, but I hadn't counted on being in the boot of their car. In fact, I had planned to be sipping a gin and tonic by now.

Confined but unrestrained in the small space, I reached up to the lid of the boot to feel for the release cable I knew should be there. In all honesty I expected them to have removed it, its sole purpose being to let a person out if ever they became *accidentally* trapped in a car's rear luggage compartment, but it wasn't there. They had removed it, which came as no surprise because I doubted I was the first person ever to get stuffed into the boot of this particular car.

Was there another way I could get it open? I felt around in the dark, knowing there would be a tool kit in here somewhere. I was in a Mercedes, I knew that much, but whether the tools and spare tyre were underneath a panel I was trapping in place with my body or not, I had no idea.

Getting nowhere in my search, I flopped onto my back and kicked at the boot catch. All that did was hurt my foot. The car went around a tight corner, but did that put me on Ryarsh Street or Ditton Lane? I was already too disorientated to tell.

Then the voices inside turned to shouts and I was propelled forward hard against the back of the rear seats as the driver slammed the brakes on, then thrown around as the car jerked into reverse and pirouetted about to face the other way.

They were going to try to escape! And I was still trapped in the boot!

Southampton

Three days before the terrifying ordeal in the boot of the car and unaware of the events ahead of me, I looked about at the Windsor Suite. My name is Patricia Fisher and the finest suite on board the world's most luxurious passenger cruise liner has been my home for the last ninety-four days, a period so long and so filling that I could barely remember a time when I wasn't staying here. Yet, to contradict myself, I could easily remember not being here. My arrival on the Aurelia was a confusing mess of overwhelming emotions that might fade as time went on but could never truly be forgotten.

Three months ago, I caught my husband of thirty years in bed with my oldest and best friend. My flight from that situation resulted in emptying all my husband's bank accounts, filling several suitcases and driving at speed to Southampton. I would love to claim that I had a plan, but mostly I had too much gin in my bloodstream to consider the idea twice and bought the stupidly expensive ticket before I knew what I was doing. Only once on board the Aurelia did the pent-up emotions finally break through the dam I had walled them behind. In the elevator, as the captain of the ship personally escorted me to my suite, they played the same song I had danced to at my wedding and it proved too much. At the realisation that I had been wasting away in an unfulfilling marriage and boring life, I sobbed into the poor man's uniform until he more or less dragged me into my suite and out of public sight.

That, over the next few weeks, I found the inner strength to drag myself out of the depths of my despair and gone on to find myself was something I could claim only a small portion of the credit for. My butler, a man appointed to the suite, had been the main reason why I could now hold my head high and feel proud of who I was. Jermaine Clarke hailed from Jamaica, he was six feet four inches tall and had the skills and reflexes of a cat genetically spliced with a ninja. He had kept me alive, kept me sane, and kept my gin and tonic topped up for the last three months. Leaving the ship and leaving him behind felt like cutting off one of my limbs. He acted in a subservient role, tending to my needs, cleaning, ironing, preparing my meals, and though I was uncomfortable with the concept of having a servant, he convinced me over time that it gave him joy. I considered him to be my dearest friend. I loved him, but in a completely platonic way. Had there been any sense of attraction on my part it would have been utterly wasted for I was almost thirty years his senior and he was gay

He wasn't the only friend I had made on this trip. Jermaine's BFF was a size zero, blonde bombshell, gym instructor called Barbara Berkeley. Everyone called her Barbie and she was incredibly sweet and loyal to a fault. I was going to miss her too.

One friend I wasn't going to miss, because she lived just a few miles from me, was Lady Mary Bostihill-Swank. She had been picked up by her helicopter an hour ago as the ship was still coming past the Isle of Wight. She offered me a lift home; she had a landing pad at her stately home and could organise getting my car collected from Southampton Docks she said. She had thought of everything, but I said no anyway. I wanted to drag my time on board out until the last possible moment. The truth was that I didn't want to get off the ship.

Having taken the captain as my lover many weeks ago, he and I had arrived at a point where he wanted me to stay on board and be his significant other. Alistair Huntley was everything most women would want, or maybe that ought to be *should* want. He was handsome, looked after himself, had never been married and carried no baggage. He had a position of power but rather than lording it over his crew, he held their respect and trust. I had seen it for myself: they loved him. And he loved me.

Which hurt.

Because I didn't love him.

I knew that I ought to. I knew that he was this perfect, once in a lifetime opportunity for eternal happiness, but I couldn't create an emotion that wasn't there. After many sleepless hours spent staring at the ceiling, asking myself why I kept telling him no, I came to the conclusion that I just wasn't ready. I was still married to someone else, even though it was very definitely over, but while that presented a barrier, the real issue was that I wanted to stand on my own two feet. It was a tired, clichéd, overused expression but one that fit my circumstances perfectly. I couldn't see myself with Alistair until I had gone through the process of working out who I was. Otherwise, I would forever be nothing more than the woman on his arm. Plus, if he really did love me, he would wait for me to work myself through this period and then, maybe, there could be a future for us. In short, I couldn't stay on board for Alistair even though he wanted me to. For Jermaine perhaps, but not for Alistair.

I sighed for about the twentieth time, looking at all the things that seemed so familiar and trying my very hardest to commit them to memory. I had photographs, of course, but I wanted to be able to see the suite with Jermaine bustling about in it when I closed my eyes rather than having to drag out an album first.

'Is there anything more I can do for you, madam?' asked Jermaine. For the last ten minutes, as I stared despairingly about the suite, he had waited patiently near the door. Anna, my bulgingly pregnant Dachshund, was asleep at my feet, the lazy creature choosing to rest whenever we stopped moving.

I sighed again, placing a hand on my chest to steady myself so that my voice wouldn't crack when I spoke. I had no desire to display how emotional I was feeling though I was certain Jermaine already knew. 'No, thank you, Jermaine. You have done so much for me already.'

'It has been my privilege, madam,' he assured me.

I felt myself about to sigh again and forced it down. I had wallowed for long enough. 'My bags have all been taken down?'

'Yes, madam. There are two porters poised to escort you to your car so that they might load it for you.' Two porters had brought my bags on board three months ago when Captain Alistair Huntley found me trying to stuff my knickers back into an exploded suitcase. I remembered the incident as clearly as if it were yesterday. Today I wondered if my tired old car would even start.

It was time to go. I twitched Anna's lead, rattling her collar which jerked her awake. 'Come along, little lady. I am going to show you England. We have the North Downs to walk upon and all manner of autumnal woodlands to visit at this time of year. It will be such an adventure.' I started toward the door and Jermaine started following me, his intention, I was sure, to follow me all the way to my car. I stopped. 'Please stay here, Jermaine,' I begged. 'I want my parting memory of you to be in this suite, not on the dreary quayside in Southampton.' His eyes met mine. 'Is that okay?'

He inclined his head. 'Whatever madam wishes.' He was doing a great job of keeping his emotions in check but as a tear leaked from my right eye, so one escaped from his left. I dropped Anna's lead and fell into his arms, my tall butler catching me as I threw myself at him.

We stayed like that for a minute or more, clinging to each other like lovers about to be torn apart forever. Finally, I patted his arm, sniffed deeply and pulled myself away, leaving the suite without a further word, little Anna trotting along beside me.

There is a private exit for the guests staying in the ship's royal suites. I had used it almost every time I came and went from the ship with the exception of a few occasions when it suited me better to leave by the crew exit. The private exit meant a slick, swift and above all traffic free route out, but today, when I could legitimately use it for the last time, I had chosen to join the throngs of people going out of the main exit. There was nothing special about me; I refused to believe that there was even though this trip had brought me some semblance of fame or notoriety. I was just an ordinary middle-aged woman. I was also about to be divorced, I had no job with which to support myself, I had no place to live and I owned a rubbish car that was unlikely to start when I turned the key.

That I had found the keys for it after three months was a miracle in itself.

I had a semblance of a plan, but that was all I could call it. Soon I would find out if the plan was worth the two minutes thought I had put into it.

The press of people ahead of me were filing out of the ship. A lot of passengers had luggage with them; English citizens returning to England. I was one of them, though my luggage was already located somewhere on the quayside waiting for me. It would throw the porters that I had chosen to leave by the riffraff exit, as so many of the royal suites' guests called it, but I would find them easily enough even as they watched the wrong gangplank.

What I didn't know was that they were not the only ones watching the exit for me. Another man was awaiting my appearance. A man I didn't know and would have shied away from had I seen him.

To my great surprise, the car started. I was prepared for a dull click as the starter motor solenoid tried to work but found it had too little amperage to throw the starter itself. Or perhaps I would get nothing at all, the key failing to raise the slightest sign of life. Defying my expectation, it roared with gusto, belching thick grey smoke from the exhaust onto the Ferrari parked behind it.

Thirty yards ahead of me, the two porters, with my luggage between them, were still watching the royal suites' exit for me to emerge. Having left by the other exit, I chose to check the car first. There was no sense in having them load it if it was dead.

I spotted the third man watching the entrance but paid him no mind. He was unusually tall and had no neck to speak of, over-developed trapezoid muscles tiering almost directly from his shoulders to his ears. I didn't know him or expect him, so my observation was in passing only.

Now that the car was running, I left it in neutral and walked over to the porters, tapping one on the shoulder. 'Hello, chaps.'

They seemed surprised to find me behind them but made no comment, dutifully collecting my bags and carrying them to my car. The slightly rusty, slightly battered Ford Fiesta sat between a Bentley Continental GT convertible which had to cost about the same as a family home and a vintage Rolls Royce Phantom. It was laughable really that I had spent three months rubbing shoulders with such people. Not that they were awful. I think that almost everyone I met was polite and decent, with a few exceptions. They were simply people with money. Many of them had made their own money, or, like Lady Mary, had inherited it from an older family member who had made it.

It was I who was the cuckoo in the nest.

I tipped the porters generously; the last two members of crew to see me that day, the last two members of the crew I would ever see, and I drove away, refusing to look in my rear-view mirror until the ship was no longer in it. Anna slept on the passenger seat, the little Dachshund indifferent to her surroundings providing she was with me which was a comfort in itself and perhaps a lesson also.

Southampton back to East Malling in Kent was not a long way to go depending on one's perspective. It took me just over two hours, the roads looking familiar for the first time in three months and unlike the drive to Southampton, which could be more accurately described as a flight, I stayed below the speed limit.

Leaving the M20 motorway at Junction Four, I was suddenly back among roads I had known my entire life, turning left and right almost without thinking until I fetched up at the bed and breakfast I had booked for myself just two days ago. I had money in my purse and money in a bank account Barbie helped me open a week ago. It wasn't a huge amount, which is a little misleading to say because it was most of the ninety-seven thousand pounds I had taken from Charlie plus the reward money from the sapphire. That sounds like a lot, even though I split the reward money with Jermaine and Barbie, but when one considers that I would probably have to give Charlie back some of the money I took from the joint accounts, and then buy a house and furnish it, it didn't amount to anywhere near enough. However, it was more than most women in my position had and sufficient to get started. I could feel sorry for myself, but what would be the point. Too many people had things far worse than me anyway, so I knew such self-indulgent emotions would be unjustified.

Mrs Crawford owned the B&B. She had for as long as I could remember. Though I knew not what her story was, I knew she was alone now because Mr Crawford had passed. East Malling was a small village; small enough that everyone knew everyone, most of the gossip being passed by Mavis the busybody at the post office. It doubled as the village store and, given our remote location, everyone went there at least once a week.

A curtain twitched as I pulled onto the drive and stopped the car; Mrs Crawford no doubt checking out who was arriving. By the time I had Anna out of the car, the front door was open and Mrs Crawford, an eighty-year-old lady with a tight grey perm and a pinafore fixed to her waist, was standing in it. She waved in recognition.

'Hello, Patricia,' she said. 'You're the talk of the village, you know.'

I sighed again. It was to be expected. My face had made it onto television and newspapers because of my exploits in Zangrabar. Heck my dog was pregnant by one of the Queen's Corgis. I possessed a pseudo-fame that I didn't want but couldn't avoid. I believed it would fade with time, but I needed to exploit it quickly first and that was the next part of the plan.

'Hello, Beatrix. Are you well?'

Mrs Crawford flipped her grey eyebrows as she turned around and beckoned me to follow, a smile playing across her face. 'My hips are a better barometer than my barometer, dear. We keep going though. A little Dunkirk spirit will see us through.' I couldn't argue. I took a similar attitude all the time: feeling sorry for oneself disrespects those who have it far, far worse.

She showed me my room; a pleasant but bland space with a double bed and a chest of drawers and a window that looked out to my car. Then she explained a few rules, like what time she locked the front door and when I could expect breakfast. There was no butler to fix me the perfect gin and tonic, no size zero gym instructor to put me through my paces and no handsome lover to make me forget everything in the world but him at that precise moment. It was just me and a heavily pregnant dog who had already started showing signs of nesting.

I had a plan though.

The Plan

I couldn't do much about the plan at Mrs Crawford's delightful B&B. There was no internet, which defied belief a little bit given the year, but there wasn't, so in order to do the next thing on my list, I needed to take a drive.

I found a pub easily enough in West Malling; the next village along. It was bigger and more populated than East Malling and had a proper high street with shops and restaurants and public houses. In a large property that quite coincidentally was able to serve me a Hendricks and tonic in a large balloon glass, I logged onto the internet and began the process of registering myself as a business owner.

The idea had come to me weeks ago. It then sat there, fermenting and stewing inside my head as I considered it, but I couldn't deny that it made sense: I was going to open a business as a private detective. I told no one, afraid of what comments they might pass and unwilling to let their opinion sway my decision. Because of that, I had no one to discuss my ideas with and had no one to blame if the name of my business was rubbish. Nervously, I entered the name I came up with: Patricia Fisher Investigation Bureau.

My finger hovered over the commit button and couldn't quite click it, so I opened a new window and searched for other private investigation agencies in the local area. I found only one, a firm in Rochester who specialised in the paranormal it seemed. Blue Moon Investigations was a silly name, I felt.

Finding no competition worth bothering with and berating myself for dithering, I jabbed the button and created my own company, jumping to the page where I paid Companies House to register me. It was exciting and exhilarating and terrifying all at the same time. It was done though. I now had my own detective agency. If I could attract a client, I would be able to call it a viable business.

I was fifty-three years old, I had no qualifications to support my intended endeavour, but I knew I could solve a mystery. Goodness knows I had unravelled a few of them recently. The first part of the plan complete, I then thought about what I wanted to do next. The swift and easy answer was that I wanted to drain my glass of gin and order another. Unfortunately, since I needed to drive my car, a second portion of gin was out of the question, so I sipped the one I had frugally, and considered what to do next. I needed a property from which I could run the business; an office of some kind. It didn't need to be large, but I felt it had to look the part if I was to sell myself as a professional investigator.

I also needed a place to live. This was an entirely different proposition because I would need a mortgage and I was on the cusp of being too old to get one and had no provable income. The latter would be a major problem.

Accepting that the new home conundrum almost certainly depended on the eventual settlement of my divorce, I chose instead to look at offices. I started in the local area and expanded my search when the price per month scared me. West Malling was a money area; I knew that, I had lived near here all my life. Its direct rail link to the centre of London planted it firmly in the commuter belt and that alone made the property prices jump.

I searched for so long that Anna started to whine, and my gin and tonic started to evaporate. I was just about to give up when I found one; a small office, a single room with an attached toilet above a travel agency in Rochester High Street. It was in a great position theoretically in that it would have a lot of passing traffic and the owner boasted that it had been completely refurbished since the last owner vacated. It was cheap too. Seriously cheap. Far cheaper than anything I had looked at so far.

I phoned the number.

It rang for long enough that I thought it wasn't going to be answered. Suddenly though, it was picked up, 'Tony Jarvis Travel, if you need a break, we're the ones to provide it.'

Ten minutes later I had an appointment to see the property the next day and an agreed price per month, if I chose to take it, that was even lower than the advertised price on the website. He came across as desperate which made me a little nervous, but I hadn't committed any money yet. With a final promise to meet him the next day, we ended the call and I placed my phone on the table.

There was nothing left in my glass except some melted water from the ice but as I stared at it, I felt good. The plan was enacted. Okay it wasn't running yet, I hadn't made a penny, but all the parts were in place. I checked the list on my phone. The next item was a business bank account. I figured that was also something I could set up quite easily, so I did, spending the next forty minutes entering information. I had to give a permanent address, so I went with what I now thought of as Charlie's house. I was registered at that address and didn't have another, nor would I anytime soon.

The screen told me the process was complete and I would receive confirmation emails soon. Satisfied, I sat back in my chair, drank the meltwater and then a new thought occurred to me: marketing. If I didn't advertise the business, then I wouldn't attract any customers. So how did I tackle that?

I thought about it for a while, found myself getting grumpy from all the things I needed to do and decided I had endured a tough enough day already. I was going to head back to the B&B, sort my things out and settle in for the evening. Anna would appreciate a walk and I would need to find a place to eat. They were all mundane and simple tasks, and each would do a good job of distracting me from the rest of my life.

Back at the B&B, I slowed my car, spying the turning and starting to turn the wheel before I spotted the gaggle of people standing in the driveway. There were dozens of them, all swinging my direction and looking excited as they burst into action. I pumped the brakes, Anna digging her claws in as her back end slid off the passenger's seat.

Cameras were clicking at me, flashes going off in the poor light under the canopy of trees and I recognised what they were even without introductions: they were reporters. They were crowding my car, jostling each other for the prime spot even though I hadn't yet parked. Anna took exception to the faces pressing toward my windows, barking and growling and showing them her teeth in a display of threat.

I had to wave my hands to get them to move, which they did eventually, still bumping and elbowing each other to be the first to get in my face. There were at least a dozen of them and though it wasn't my first time ever talking to reporters, I got lots of it in Zangrabar, I really didn't feel able to handle them right now.

With Anna scooped under my left arm so she wouldn't bite anyone and go into premature labour, I shoved the door open with my shoulder and tried to get out. Tried is the right word too because they were surrounding the door, blocking my path to the house so there was no way to escape them.

A microphone was thrust toward my face. 'Mathew Jenkins, Kent Chronicle. What's it like to be back home, Patricia? Will you be going away again? Is it true you were involved in a love triangle with the teenage

Maharaja of Zangrabar?' Anna lunged forward and bit the microphone, growling viciously as she tried to rip it from his hands.

Another microphone came over his shoulder, an arm stretching to get it near my mouth. 'Mrs Fisher, a word for The Weald Word? Will you be continuing your mystery solving now that you are back here? Will you join the police?'

I moved my head forward as if I intended to speak, then snatched the microphone from the rude man's hand and threw it into a bush.

'Right, you lot.' I narrowed my eyes as I addressed the unruly crowd pressing in from all sides. 'I have been back in this country for a number of hours only. I haven't unpacked my clothes, I haven't spoken to anyone, and I am not giving anyone an interview today.' I saw the opportunity for free advertising though, so I said, 'You can hand me a business card and be on your way. I will be in contact when I am ready.'

A young woman, small enough to squeeze through the gap, went under the arms of the men all around me and popped up right in front of me with a handheld recording device. 'Mrs Fisher, are you working on a case right now? Will you clean up the streets of England?'

The first man had his microphone working again, the visible chew mark on the end of it not affecting its function. 'Can you tell us how it is that a woman with no discernible skills or training, a woman who until three months ago was cleaning houses for a living, becomes a famous sleuth?'

I slammed the car door shut, the metal on metal noise loud even with the reporters' constant babble. They weren't going to leave me in peace, but I wasn't going to cave and give them what they wanted either, so I walked forward, actually knocking the man with the chewed microphone over when he didn't move to let me pass.

With a gap in the line, I pushed through, stepping over the surprised reporter as he hit the ground. 'You will find that I mean what I say. Put your business cards in the letterbox. I will collect them later.' At my retreating back they hurled a few more questions but fell silent once I got inside.

'Will there be much of that, love?' asked Mrs Crawford, standing in the doorway to her kitchen.

She didn't look upset at the intrusion of reporters; perhaps she thought it would be good for business. 'How did they know I was here?' I asked.

'Oh, I expect Mavis at the post office told someone. You know how all the gossip in the village circulates through the post office.'

'How did Mavis know I was here?'

'Well, I told her that, love. It's not often I get famous people staying here, even if you did used to be just Patricia, the girl who wet her knickers at the church fete.'

I raised an eyebrow at her. 'That was in 1971. I don't think it needs bringing up again.'

'Well, what I mean is, you're famous now, but I suppose everyone famous had to have come from humble beginnings. You used to wet your knickers.'

'Everyone used to wet their knickers. I was four.'

'Yes, love,' she replied, not exactly agreeing with me. 'Would you like a cup of tea?'

I opened my mouth to tell her Jermaine would make one and knew exactly how I liked it but caught myself before the words came. Feeling instantly sad, I told her, 'No, thank you,' and trudged to my room.

Lying on my bed, staring at the ceiling with Anna snoring like a deranged beast under my right arm, I forced my thoughts back to the plan. Now that my business was set up and I had a bank account, I could charge people for my services. It was a little terrifying, mostly because I still felt that I had solved the cases on the ship by blind luck each time. I fell over the clues that led me to work out who had done what and why, but telling myself I was going to fail had always pushed me onward to somehow succeed. This was no different, I whispered to myself. It was no different and I already had a case.

I was going to work out why someone killed my former best friend.

Maggie's Murder

When my soon-to-be ex-husband, Charlie, contacted me ten days ago, he had the daft idea that I would curtail my trip and fly immediately home to help him. I was curious enough about the case to want to know what had happened, but the police were investigating, and I had no reason to believe they would fail to determine why she had been murdered and by whom.

He got upset when I refused to fly home from Gibraltar, the ship's next port of call, but sensing that he could only push me so far before I hung up the phone, he instead asked if I would investigate the case once I was home. I agreed that I would, if the police hadn't already solved it, but then told him I would be charging him for the pleasure. The concept shocked him, but the idea of going into business as a private investigator had been buzzing about in my head for a little while by then. With his phone call, I had a case to get me started.

In fact, I had already started looking into her murder and seeing what information I could find while I was still on board the Aurelia. Barbie and Jermaine helped me, they were both such whizzes on the computer compared to me, though I told neither of my plan to open my own firm.

Unfortunately, there wasn't much information to find. Maggie Lynn Jeffries was found by her cleaner, Emily Walker, with a single gunshot wound to her head at her home in West Malling. The time of death was late evening and she had been alone in the house, a single glass of red wine found next to her slumped body. There was no suicide note, the killer showing no interest in attempting to confuse the police, and it sounded more like an execution than a murder. Nothing was taken from the house; the police found jewellery in her bedroom plus cash in her handbag and she was still wearing one carat diamond earrings.

So, what had motivated such a crime? Someone had chosen to kill her and then performed the task with ruthless efficiency. Now, since the police hadn't been able to make an arrest yet, I was going to look into it. I had a case and I had a client. I supposed that I ought to be celebrating. That would be unseemly though, so I fished out my phone and called Charlie instead.

'Patricia, are you back?' He launched into a question straight away.

'Yes, Charlie. We docked this morning. I'm calling to discuss Maggie's case and whether you want me to take it on or not.' If he said no at this point, I was probably going to pursue it anyway until a paying case came along. It would keep me busy if nothing else.

'Um, yes, I think so. Where are you staying?'

'You don't need to know that, Charlie. If you hired any other detective, you wouldn't ask them for their home address.'

'I might,' he argued weakly. 'Anyway, I want to know who killed her and why. The police are useless.'

I rolled my eyes. 'It's only been a few days, Charlie. These things take time.'

'Not for you they don't. You solved that thing in Japan in two days.' He had me there.

'Nevertheless, each case is different, and I cannot guarantee a result quickly or at all. You need to understand that before you hire me.'

'I need to know your rate too,' he pointed out since the last time he asked I refused to tell him because I had no idea what I should charge. I had done a little research since then though and was quite impressed at what I could earn. I told him my daily rate and he swore. Several times.

'I could charge more,' I assured him. Here's the thing about being married for so many years – I knew him. I knew he was about to decide that he didn't want to have me take the case on after all and would tell me it was because he couldn't afford it. I also knew what he earned, so it wouldn't be because he couldn't afford it, but because he didn't want to give me the money. Unfortunately for Charlie, I also knew how to twist his arm. Above all else, he was cheap, so if he thought he was getting a bargain, he would snap my arm off. 'I'll tell you what, Charlie. Just for old times sake, I'll drop the fee by fifty percent.'

'Thank you, Patricia. I knew you would be reasonable.' All I had done was double what I wanted to charge him, scared him and come back in at a rate I believed I could charge. 'At the first rate, I'm not sure I would be able to afford the divorce.'

I couldn't tell if that was a joke or not, but it linked us nicely to a subject we needed to discuss. 'We need to talk about that as well, Charlie. I have no desire to get solicitors involved and make this drag out for months. I shall need to interview you for the case, take an initial payment and have you sign some paperwork. Can I come over in the morning? We can talk about how we divide our assets too.'

'What? Oh, yes. Yes, I suppose so. I will take a half day off. What time do you want to get here?'

Mrs Crawford served breakfast from six provided the lodgers expressed they wanted it that early. I would be up that early because I wanted to keep up my regime of exercise, but breakfast could wait until seven. 'How about eight o'clock?'

We agreed on eight and finished the call. I was still lying on my bed, but it was gone Anna's dinner time and all my bags were in the car still. I didn't plan to unpack it all just yet; most of it had gone into the boot or was hidden under a blanket on the back seat so I didn't worry that it might get stolen. I needed some toiletries and a few clothing options which were neatly packed into one small bag because I expected this. Tonight, I would start looking for somewhere to live, perhaps finding a small rental until the divorce came through and I could see just what money I had to buy my own place with.

I felt that I had already done a lot with my day, but then gave myself a mental slap; I wouldn't solve a case by telling myself I had worked hard enough and deserved a break. I needed to get on with things.

Peering around the side of the curtain, I could see the reporters were no longer outside, so I grabbed my bag from the boot of the car, dashed back inside in case one of them was hiding in a bush and then dashed back to the car because I had forgotten Anna's bag of things. Her items were packed into her basket on the back seat of my car. Toys, bowls, food, and all that jazz, but light enough for me to carry as one load because she is only a tiny dog.

Fifteen minutes later, she was fed and watered, and I had on a completely different outfit and a ballcap to hide my hair. It was stuffed on over a hoody which I hoped would hide my face so people wouldn't recognise me. I didn't even want anyone to see me if possible because I was about to do something naughty: I was going to break into Maggie's house.

Breaking and Entering

I was calling it breaking and entering, but I had a key so all I was really doing was entering. I wasn't sure where I stood legally, which was a failing on my part and I made a mental note to devote some time to studying law. The bits where it might apply to me, at least.

Anna needed a walk, and it was less than two miles from Mrs Crawford's bed and breakfast to Maggie's opulent oast house. The key to her house was on my bunch of keys, so I had it with me already, a happy coincidence really, but I didn't think I had ever used it. Maggie always gave me a key to her house when she bought a new place. Houses had followed divorces generally, moving up the property ladder and buying bigger places each time even though she lived by herself, and didn't have so much as a cat to share it with.

The evening was drawing in. Now that we were in early autumn, the days were far shorter already and it was twilight by the time I reached her drive. It was early summer the last time I stood on this spot and it struck me how different the trees and shrubs looked now.

Anna pulled me forward up her drive, tugging her lead as if she knew our destination was Maggie's house. I glanced about to see if there was anyone around to see me but doing so probably just made me look furtive. Besides, this was the countryside, there probably wasn't a person within two hundred yards of me, where the nearest neighbour could be found.

Telling myself to look like I belonged here, I walked confidently up to the door and opened it with the key. It swung silently inward as I pushed it. Was it better to leave it open or would that attract attention if a neighbour went by? I shut it, and then tussled with whether I should turn the lights on or not.

Deciding that I looked less guilty of anything if I turned them on and acted like I was supposed to be here, I reached for the switch to light up the lobby, wondering if a dead person still had electricity. She did, I discovered when I was bathed in light a moment later.

I knew from reading reports online a week ago that she had been killed in her office. It was on the ground floor at the back of the house where she had her desk positioned to look out over her garden. She admitted, during lunch several years ago, that her reason for the view over the garden was the young male gardener she hired. He wore nothing on his top half for about half the year and she was happy to be distracted from her work by watching him clip her shrubs topless.

The house looked exactly like it had every other time I had been here. It was spotlessly clean because she had a cleaner and looked like it belonged in a country house magazine. The mix of period features, such as an inglenook fireplace, balanced perfectly with the ultra-modern, sleek lines of her furniture and entertainment systems.

It was hard to convince myself that she wasn't about to appear through a doorway, but the dark stain on the carpet in her office drove home that she wouldn't. A cleaning crew had dealt with the worst of it, but I imagined replacing carpet and whatever else had to happen before it was sold would get worked out when someone inherited her estate. I had no idea who that might be though; she had no family that I was aware of, not even a cousin since both her parents had been only children just as she had.

None of that was of interest though, I was here to look for clues. Standing in the middle of her office and wriggling my nose about as I tried to work out where to look, the unwelcome voice in my head popped up again to remind me that I didn't know what I was doing and never had. I knew it was right, but solving mysteries hadn't been all luck. I had worked out quite a bit of it myself, I argued.

The desk drawers revealed nothing of interest, which could be because the police had already taken it all. There were no Post-It notes with map coordinates on them, no notepads with the indentation of the previous note to tell me why she had been killed, no scraps of half-burnt crumpled paper in the fireplace which I could carefully unravel to find a name that might lead me onwards. There was nothing at all. This had to be because it was a ten-day old crime scene and every scrap of evidence had been catalogued and removed by the crime scene guys, making it very different to every crime scene I had been to previously. On the ship, I usually found myself at the crime scene while the murder victim was still warm.

Undefeated, I left the office and looked around the other rooms downstairs before moving up to her bedroom; the scene of a very different crime. Standing in her doorway, I could remember the look on Charlie's face as he stood there trying to come up with an excuse for being in her bedroom with his clothes off. It was laughable now, and though it still hurt, I was glad it had happened. I poked around in her wardrobes and her drawers, slightly worried about what odd sex toys I might find, but my heart wasn't really in it anymore. I was coming to accept that there was nothing here to find, but just as I thought that, I spotted something that stopped me. On a piece of paper at the bottom of the top drawer of her bedside table was the name C. Fisher.

When I pulled it out from under the assorted paraphernalia, I saw instantly that it was a Companies House document. I had been on Companies House today to register my business and I recognised the logo. My eyes flashed left to right over the lines of the document, a single page change of address record. I knew enough about the subject to know that the directors of a business had to be registered at Companies House and had to have a registered home address. They were responsible for the finances of the firm and divided the profits.

So why was Charlie's name on it? He was registered as an executive director of Maggie's company which meant he was responsible for, but wasn't taking an active part in, the daily business dealings. The change of address document was from when Maggie last moved, which was twelve years ago.

I was going to kill him.

Anna barked unexpectedly in the silence of Maggie's house, making me jump and squeal at the same time. I spun around to yell at her but before I could speak, I heard what had caused her reaction.

There was someone downstairs.

Local Interest

Someone turned out to be lots of someones as the sound of heavy footfalls could be heard charging up the spiral staircase. I had to quickly lunge to grab Anna before she could tear off to intercept them. I wanted to hide, but Anna's bark had undoubtedly already given our presence away, which only left escape as an option.

I ran to the windows. Peering out into the now dark garden. I could get the window open. I might even be able to spot a half decent place to land and not break my legs, but I couldn't do either thing before the people now running along the upstairs hallway found me.

Was it Maggie's killer returned with friends to see if a new danger had presented itself? What had she got herself mixed up in that had caused her death and would I ever find out if this was her killers returning? Hugging Anna to my chest, I turned to face the door, disbelief washing through me that this could be the end after all I had been through on the Aurelia.

A figure burst through the doorway, making me jump again even though I knew it was coming. A second followed it but at that point the information from my eyes managed to fight past the terror in my brain and my pulse relaxed. They were cops.

Both men wore police uniform, the black making them look like shadows for a half second as they came into the room. Each had their baton raised and ready, expecting a hardened criminal not a middle-aged woman, but they raised their free hands toward me in a don't-move gesture as the one on the left said, 'Don't move.'

I smiled at him and said, 'Hello.' Then I looked at his partner and almost laughed. 'Hello, Joshua.' Joshua's eyes went wide in surprise at being named. 'You used to deliver my newspapers. I didn't know you had joined the police.'

Both men glanced at each other and visibly relaxed their tight expressions, lowering their arms as they accepted that I presented no threat. Anna was struggling to get out of my arms, she wanted to see the two new men – they might have food! I plopped her on the carpet, keeping a tight hold on her lead so she couldn't choose to attack them and sat on the end of the bed as the adrenalin seeped back out of my body.

'Mrs Fisher, isn't it?' asked the one who wasn't Joshua. 'I recognise you from the television. You know this is breaking and entering, don't you?'

'What happened here?' I asked, ignoring his questions, but giving him an engaging smile. 'You both gave me quite the scare. Where is Maggie?' My question caught them both by surprise and they exchanged another glance. They couldn't tell that I knew she was dead, so I had chosen to bluff my way out. I had been back for less than twelve hours which they would know if they knew me from the television, and people hereabouts would corroborate that Maggie was my childhood friend.

It was Joshua who answered me, 'Mrs Fisher, this is a crime scene. Did you not see the tape across the door when you came in?' I hadn't actually because it wasn't there. I didn't know whether local kids had stolen it, thinking it would be a cool thing to put around their bedroom doors, or if it had just blown away on the breeze, but I hadn't needed to duck around or under it.

Doing my best attempt at acting shocked, I gasped and put my hand to my mouth. 'Crime scene! What happened?'

Their radios squawked; a burst of static followed by a voice asking something I couldn't make out. It prompted Not-Joshua to turn away as he leaned his chin down to speak into the microphone on his lapel.

Abandoned by his colleague as he left the room, Joshua grimaced in discomfort, then crossed the room and came down on one knee in a classic proposal pose so he could get his face to eye level with mine. He had grown a lot since I last saw him poking rolled up newspapers through my door. Then he had been a scrawny teenager, all limbs and a pimply chin. Now he wore a beard and had put on thirty pounds of muscle. Local gossip being what it was, I figured I ought to have known he was the local bobby, yet it had escaped me.

With a sigh he said, 'Mrs Fisher, I'm afraid your friend is dead.'

I gasped again, milking my performance for all it was worth. 'Oh, no! I had no idea!'

'Yes, you did, Mrs Fisher.' The voice calling me a liar came from the doorway, where a new person was standing. Unlike the two uniformed cops, this fellow wore a suit. It was badly fitting, giving him a scruffy look, but I guessed instantly that he was a detective. He had more to say. 'You have been hired by your husband to look into what happened to her and why. That's right, isn't it?'

At the man's accusation, Joshua's eyes flared, and I chose to drop the pretence; I wasn't one for lying, though it had seemed like a good idea at the time. 'How do you know that already?'

I caught a brief glimpse of a wry smile. 'I went into the post office to buy milk an hour ago.' The damned post office. Everyone in the village knew everything about everyone because of Mavis in the post office. 'Mrs Jeffries slept with your husband, didn't she?' He wasn't asking a question.

'Had you not been very firmly out of the country, I might have considered you a suspect.'

The detective hadn't bothered to introduce himself yet, which I thought quite rude. Everyone knew my name, my anonymity stolen away during my cruise, yet of the three police officers I could only name one. He was short for a man, barely any taller than me I judged at perhaps five feet eight inches. He looked to be late fifties and his face bore a tiredness which suggested he had been beaten down by his life and was now getting through each day just by going through the paces. His jacket hung from his shoulders, a size too big as if he lost weight recently, which might be the case as his trousers looked big on him too. He had a bit of a belly but not much and his hair was trying hard to recede.

Thankfully, the next time he opened his mouth, it was to introduce himself. 'I'm Detective Sergeant Atwell, Mike Atwell. I was assigned to this case.'

'Was assigned?'

'Yes, it has been taken over by an organised crime unit working out of London. My boss told me that was all I needed to know.' Organised crime? What on earth had Maggie got herself mixed up in? 'I think it best if we leave the premises now, Mrs Fisher. I'm afraid we will have to deal with the breaking and entering though.'

I fished out my bunch of keys. 'I didn't break in. If you know about Maggie and my husband, then you must know she and I have been friends for almost fifty years.'

He nodded. 'I did know, yes. Having a key doesn't make it okay though. What did you do with the crime scene tape?'

'There wasn't any,' I assured him.

He glanced at Joshua and pursed his lips. Then beckoned me from the room with his right arm. 'Come along, Mrs Fisher. It is time to leave.'

I didn't think I could argue, and I didn't think I could come back either. However, there was nothing here for me to find since they had cleared the house of any clues. It had been worth the visit though because the one slip of paper I did find told me why Charlie was so interested in having me solve the case. That might prove useful and maybe he would know what she was mixed up in. He was going to get grilled anyway.

I was escorted from the bedroom and down the stairs, the two uniforms bookending me as if I was a dangerous criminal. At the door, DS Atwell, stopped me and held out his right hand. 'The key, please, Mrs Fisher. We'll say nothing about it this time, but if I catch you in here again...'

'You won't.' I brushed by him, placing the key in his hand without looking and found myself back outside where the sun had fully set to leave the garden in darkness. The outside lights hadn't come on with my movement, telling me they were switched off inside already. 'How did you know I was here?' I asked, suddenly curious.

DS Atwell joined me on the gravel driveway. 'The alarm is still on and the alarm firm have instructions to call us.' He scratched his chin, which let me see the lack of wedding ring on his finger. I was curious about the local detective. I might need to know him if I was going to be investigating cases in this area. 'Can I trust you to behave, Mrs Fisher? I can't stop you from doing what apparently you do very well, but I have to advocate against you breaking any laws. You have no special rights as a private investigator, if that is what you are now.'

I narrowed my eyes at him. 'I am well aware of what I can and cannot do, thank you. Someone needs to find out what happened to my friend though and it doesn't seem that you will be doing it.'

He gave me an innocent expression. 'I'm following orders, Mrs Fisher. If Chief Inspector Quinn wants me to ignore the case so some special task force in the city can look into it, then that's what I am going to do. It's back to missing garden gnomes and stolen shopping trolleys for me.'

I couldn't tell if he was being flippant or was happy to take on the mundane local crimes. Either way, it didn't matter. He wasn't involved in Maggie's case and wouldn't be able to give me any information.

I bade him good evening and started to walk away. He caught up to me after a few steps, while the uniforms made sure the house was secure. 'Of course, if a certain lady with an interest in the case wanted to ask me a few questions over a coffee and then happened to solve the murder before the idiots in London, there wouldn't be much the Chief Inspector could do about that, would there?'

My jaw dropped open slightly in surprise. He was offering to share what he knew about the case. I didn't know who Chief Inspector Quinn was, though DS Atwell clearly bore sufficient animosity toward him to want to deliberately undermine his efforts. Gathering myself, I asked, 'When might you be free for a coffee?'

'Some time tomorrow?' He reached into a coat pocket to pull out a card. 'Call me when you are free. I'm sure I can steal myself away from another terrible case of littering in the park.'

My assessment of the man had changed completely in thirty seconds. I thanked him, promised to call tomorrow, a day which was fast filling with tasks and appointments, and started back toward Mrs Crawford's bed and breakfast. Then I caught myself and called to get his attention before he could get to his car. 'The other officer, the one that isn't Joshua, what's his name please?'

'PC Marvin Gaye.' I raised an eyebrow. 'His name isn't Marvin obviously, but that's what he gets called by everyone. I have no idea what his real name is.'

I waved him goodnight and he tipped an imaginary hat in return. A rumble from my tummy reminded me that I hadn't eaten so I set myself a winding detour that would take me to the post office. The post office bit of the local store wouldn't be open at this time of the day, but I would be able to buy a sandwich and that would do for tonight.

In the morning, I was going to have a conversation with Charlie that he wouldn't enjoy.

The next morning, Charlie looked pleased to see me when he opened the door. I was going to change that soon enough. 'Hello, Patricia, welcome back. Come in, come in.'

He stepped back to allow me access to my own house. I wasn't sure what I expected to find but devastation had been top of the list. Charlie had never been one for cleaning up after himself; I wasn't even sure he could find the vacuum cleaner, yet the house was spotless.

'Do you have a cleaner?' I asked.

'Yes,' he chuckled. 'I could never manage to keep the old place looking like this by myself. I don't know how you ever managed it.'

I sighed in irritation. 'You just tackle a bit of it every day, or you commit a few hours to it once a week, Charlie. It's not hard.' I felt myself being pulled into a familiar old argument and reigned myself in before it happened.

'Yes, well,' he replied, a little snippily. 'Emily does it now. She's very efficient and very cheap.'

'Emily? The same woman who used to clean Maggie's place?'

'Err, yes,' he admitted, his face colouring slightly. 'That's where I got her from. After you left, the place got a bit scruffy since there was no one to clean it. I mentioned it to Maggie, and she gave me Emily's number.'

His infidelity with Maggie felt very present now that I was home again, and I dearly wanted to have a go at him for it. I had a bigger weapon to use though. 'What year did you become a director at Maggie's firm?' His panicked look told me everything I wanted to know about that particular secret: I was never supposed to know. 'How much money do you have invested in it?' I got no answer to my second question either, his brain scrambling for a safe place to hide. 'Were you sleeping with her when the two of you decided to go into business together?'

'Goodness, no, Patricia,' he protested, but stopped talking when I held my hand in front of his face.

'I can't believe a word you tell me, Charlie Fisher, so there is no point denying any of it. You invested money in a business without discussing it with your wife at any point. Just how much money was it?'

'Not much,' he mumbled.

'How much?' My words came out with fire on them. I was livid that I had lived my life as a cleaner and driven a tatty, battered car while he was investing money and making secret deals. Of course, I didn't have to work as a cleaner and could have stamped my foot until I had a better car, so some of the blame was mine. But he should have treated me better so that making a fuss was never necessary. Pointing the finger at him felt better though.

'I put in twenty-five thousand when she first opened the business in 1998. The shares are worth considerably more than that now. It was a very astute investment. You were even there when she and I discussed it.' I shook my head in disbelief. Sensing an opening, he pressed on. 'It was at a dinner party here. She was talking about seeing a better way of running the publishing business and about setting up on her own. She said she needed seed money to get it off the ground.' Now I saw his confusion. Charlie often used to throw dinner parties, he thought they were a sophisticated thing to do and he often invited bosses and persons of influence to help him grease his way up the slippery corporate pole. It worked for him, but he missed that I spent two days preparing for them and all night running around filling drinks and doing my best to feed twelve people a five-course dinner. He always acted like announcing he had invited a stack of people should fill me with joy. I always invited Maggie, usually at his request because she was attractive and almost always single.

We were off topic now though. 'Tell me the real reason why you want me to investigate her murder, Charlie.' I jabbed him in the chest with my index finger.

I thought he was going to start lying again, but he drew in a deep breath and let his shoulders slump as if deflating while he accepted defeat. 'I think she was mixed up in some kind of organised crime. The police asked me a bunch of questions about her business affairs because I am the other named director. I couldn't tell them anything though, I have always been a silent partner, never involved in what was happening. I was content to collect my dividend cheque each year, but I never involved myself in what she was doing. I don't know anything about the publishing industry.'

'Did the police suggest that she might have been killed by an organised crime gang?'

He shook his head. 'No, they wouldn't really tell me anything. They asked me if I had ever heard from a man called Jim Brevin or a man called Ian Drummond. I told them I hadn't but when I looked them up, I found they are known leaders of an East End gang called the Old City Firm.' He looked down at the carpet, shrugged to himself and looked up again to meet my eyes. 'I'm worried they killed her for something to do with the firm and they might be after me next. The police told me to be vigilant.'

'Did they also tell you not to worry?'

'They did, but I figured they had to say that, or I really would worry.' Now my mind was racing. The cops were most likely just being cautious in telling Charlie to be on the lookout. If they were genuinely worried, they would have placed someone to watch over him. That they hadn't made me want to believe that he was unlikely to be connected. Charlie was worried enough to contact me though and I frowned deeply as I sensed that he still wasn't telling me everything.

'There's more, Charlie. You have to remember that I know what a dirty little weasel you are.'

He tried to look hurt. 'Hey, steady on, Patricia.'

My stony look stopped him from saying anything else. 'You lied to me for years about investments and kept squirreling the money away. Where is it? Some offshore account I don't know about?' I saw the truth register in his eyes. 'There's no good protesting that you are not guilty, Charles. You know more than you are telling me and, so help me, if you don't start telling me the truth soon, I will hire a divorce lawyer who will tear you apart.'

He held up both hands in surrender, looking very much like he was about to fall to his knees and beg for mercy. 'I don't know much. Honest,' he added when I narrowed my eyes at him again. 'The office manager is a chap called Mathew Hughes. He runs the whole operation out of an office close to Trafalgar Square. I only met him once, but he has been running the show for years. Maggie wanted to be less involved, I guess, and hiring a manager allowed her to effectively retire in her forties.'

'And?'

'Well, I haven't been able to get hold of him and the people who are answering their phones at the office told me he hasn't been seen for a couple of weeks.'

'A couple of weeks? How long is it exactly?'

He looked upward into his skull as he calculated. 'Twelve days including today. He vanished right before Maggie was killed.' The police had to know this already. The first thing they would have checked out was her job and all the people she knew.

'He's not answering his phone?' I sought to confirm.

'No. He doesn't know my number though so it could be that he is just ignoring my calls.' I finally got the sense that Charlie was telling me the truth. Mathew Hughes was a person of interest, but that meant the police would be looking for him as well. If he was still alive, he had gone on the run and was hiding out somewhere. Maybe I would be able to find him. A trip to Maggie's office would get me some more detail on his life.

Charlie didn't know anything more about the man, so I moved on. 'How was her business doing?' I asked. I always got the impression she was rolling in money, but it could have been a façade.

'Very well. The business had positive growth year on year of between ten and thirty percent. The return on investment...' I held up a hand to slow him down.

'I don't need a full fiscal picture, Charlie. I'm just trying to work out what the gangster connection is. What I am hearing is that she was making good money and rarely went to the office. Her opportunity to get mixed up with organised crime ought to have been almost nil which makes me think it was someone else in the business, most likely Mathew Hughes, who was guilty of that connection. I will find out. What else can you tell me about her? Who was she involved with? You told me she dumped you as soon as I found out.'

'That's right,' he admitted glumly. 'She wasn't actually interested in me other than for sex.' His cheeks were red when he realised what he was telling me. I was way past caring though. Bringing his embarrassment under control, he said, 'I think she was seeing several men. I couldn't tell you who though. I saw a number of different cars parked at her house whenever I went past.'

'Makes and models. I need a list.' I started walking through the house to the kitchen at the back. There he could sit at the table and write me a list of cars. It might be nothing, but it was another starting point. He trailed after me to slump reluctantly into a chair when I clicked my fingers and pointed. He didn't have registration numbers, but he was very good at remembering cars and colours, quickly producing a list of ten cars, most of them rather nice ones, with one very obvious exception.

I pointed to the last car on the list, a silver Renault Clio. It looked incongruous on the list of BMWs, Bentleys and Jaguars. 'Oh,' he said, putting a line through it. 'That's Emily's car. I'm pretty sure Maggie wasn't sleeping with her.' I didn't want to comment on Maggie's tastes, but I took the list and placed it in my handbag.

'Did she ever talk about anyone wanting to hurt her. Was she ever afraid of anyone?' I kept on with the questions for another half an hour but got very little information from him. She used him for sex, their relationship starting almost a year before I found out, but they didn't talk much and despite being the original business investor and a named director for the firm, he knew very little about that either. She had tried to buy him out several times he admitted. She had more than enough money to do so and didn't like that she had to keep on paying him for his part in getting the business off the ground.

Exhausting my list of questions, I switched to the next subject: our divorce.

'I want to keep the house,' he announced as soon as I raised the subject. 'You already moved out and...'

I held up my hand. 'I don't want the house. I will buy somewhere new to live.' He looked relieved. 'I expect an amicable split of our assets though. Every court in the land will award me half or more, since you are the adulterous one,' I paused to give him a chance to argue, but he surprised me by keeping his mouth shut. 'That's all I want, Charlie. Half. That means you will need to have the house valued and give me half of what they think it is worth.'

'I already did that,' he replied. This was good. Charlie had most likely investigated his position to ascertain what he could get away with and accepted that he would be lucky to get away with half. For the next hour, we looked at bank accounts, items of furniture, record collections and other insignificant items. I let him have almost all of it. There were things that were mine, but I didn't feel any attachment to the things in our house; he could keep them. I would find my own place and fill it with my own things, which would include towels and bedding that an adulterous husband hadn't touched before me. It seemed like such a silly thing, but I never wanted to touch the same linen as him again; it would feel tainted.

When I left his house, I had a deposit for my services in my brand-new business bank account and a signature on the contract I bought as a template from an online shop that sold such things. I could get better ones later, but it said he had engaged my services and agreed to pay me a set daily rate. All the information was on the contract and I felt organised and ready to go now that it was signed.

Back in my car, I thought about which task to tackle next. I needed to go to the post office, visit the potential office for my business in Rochester High Street, and call DS Atwell to arrange a chat with him during which I hoped to learn everything he knew about Maggie's murder and really accelerate my investigation.

The post office was closest, so I went there first.

Post Office

I had several reasons for visiting the post office, the first of which was food. Breakfast at Mrs Crawford's was pleasant enough, but her full English fry up with all the trimmings wasn't going to do my waistline any good no matter how many miles I ran beforehand. The village store had fruit and other healthy items I could buy and that would keep me going for a couple of days until I found a place to rent and could stock a kitchen. I also wanted to speak with Mavis, the village gossip, who had worked in the post office for several decades. In such a small village as East Malling everyone knew everyone anyway, but Mavis prided herself on knowing everything about everyone and was only too pleased to reveal anything she knew. Always dropping her voice to reveal the big secret as if the information was just for you and she wasn't going to tell the next two hundred people coming through the shop. If there were things to know, she would know them.

On my way there, a clunking noise came from under my bonnet. Then the car backfired and died. Muttering with dread, I coasted to a stop at the side of the road with my hazard lights on and got out to have a look. With the bonnet up, I looked down at the engine. 'Well, that's an engine,' I muttered to myself because that was as far as my knowledge went. I could top up the washer jet fluid and I knew which bit was the battery. After that, it was all a mystery too complicated for me to solve. It wasn't smoking or on fire, so I closed the bonnet again and tried the key. To my amazement, it started, so I tentatively pulled away and made it the rest of the way to the post office without further incident. I chalked it up to a mechanical hiccup and promised to get the old girl serviced soon – another item to add to my already long list.

Inside the door, it took about half a second for Mavis to recognise me and speak loudly enough for everyone in the store to hear, 'The wanderer returns.' Mavis Cruet had never been married and, to my knowledge, had never left the village. For her a trip to Maidstone six miles away was an adventure beyond comprehension. She had half a dozen cats or more; always on the windowsill of her house when I passed it, sleeping on top of one another and making a mess of her net curtains. She was in her early sixties and had taken a part time job at the local store when she was fourteen and never looked back. She didn't bother with makeup or fashion or hairstyling products and I didn't think I had ever seen her in any footwear other than wellies. I suspect that every village has a Mavis lurking in it somewhere, the kind of person you are polite to but avoid if you can.

I flipped my eyebrows. Mavis never had been quiet, or tactful, or respecting of other people's boundaries. I should have expected her to trumpet my arrival. 'Yes, hello, Mavis,' I replied as I made my way to the post office counter. There were two women in front of me, but she ignored them both to speak to me. 'Are you back for good? I understand you are staying at Mrs Crawford's.' She turned to the two ladies, 'Won't keep you a minute, ladies, we have someone famous in.'

'What? Patricia Fisher?' The two old ladies were Margaret Callaghan and Hope Lashley, both women of the village and both widowed in their seventies. Now in their eighties they trundled about together, playing canasta and knitting dolls for the church to sell.

'Ridiculous, isn't it,' I agreed quickly, keen to show that I didn't think I was famous at all.

Mavis wasn't done though. 'Will you be divorcing that Charlie of yours? We all heard about him and Maggie Jeffries. She always was trouble, that one, God rest her soul. Quite the maneater though. I hear you're going to be investigating it.'

She finally stopped talking so I could get a word in. 'Yes, that's right.' Mavis was waiting for me to say more, to give her some juicy tidbit about the case so I took joy in denying her that pleasure. It might make her hungrier for information which I could milk to get her to tell me what she knew. She was staring at me and still ignoring her customers, Margaret huffing loudly, not that it made any difference. I winked at Mavis. 'Perhaps you should serve these ladies and then the two of us can have a proper catch up.'

Her eyes lit up and then her hands became a flurry of activity as she dealt with their pension payments and post and shooed them on their way. Then, with Margaret and Hope muttering loudly as they shuffled toward the door, Mavis leaned on the counter to give me her undivided attention. I leaned in too, getting my face close to the glass that separated us. 'Can you keep a secret?' I asked.

Mavis blew out a surprised breath, 'Goodness, yes, of course.' I was just teasing her. Mavis's inability to keep anything secret was legendary.

'First, tell me what you know about Maggie's business, who she was seen with, who visited her house and who you think she might have been sleeping with.' I laid my phone on the counter near the little speaking grill and set it to record voice. I could make notes later but wouldn't be able to keep up now. It took no time for Mavis to start reeling off names and dates and other bits of information which might prove pertinent. She was a mine of information as I had expected her to be. She let slip that she had known about Maggie's affair with my husband long before I found out, though she failed to notice the faux pas and I let it go without comment. Maggie had an extraordinarily long list of lovers according to Mavis though how much of what she told me was reliable and how much was gossip I couldn't judge. She told me about a young man she had seen in the village several times recently. When prompted to define what she meant by young, she clarified it as anyone under forty. She told me he drove a vintage Aston Martin, which when tallied against the list of cars Charlie wrote placed him as an almost certain visitor of Maggie's. She gave me a description too; bookish, she said, glasses, a bit weedy, by which I assume she meant he was lean rather than carrying excess weight, but again he wore a nice suit and gave her the impression he had money. Then she said, 'He worked for her, you know.'

'How can you tell?'

'He had to send a card A birthday card to his mother which he bought here in the shop and came to the counter to get a stamp. He wrote it out at the counter where you are standing and used a pen with her business name on it. Jeffries Imperial Publishing. That's her firm.' She was right, it was. Did that mean the man she described was Mathew Hughes. Using the phone, I pulled up a picture of him to show her. 'That's him,' she confirmed. 'Very polite young man.'

So, Mathew Hughes was coming to Maggie's house on a regular basis if Mavis was to be believed. It could be entirely innocent; he worked for her after all and maybe she decided she wanted him to report to her rather than making the trip to the office herself. I had largely tuned Mavis out as I thought, but then she said something which caught my attention. 'Can you say again, please?'

'There was a man in here looking for you earlier this morning. He came in yesterday too. Big ugly looking brute he is too.'

'Did he say what he wanted?' I really didn't like the sound of this.

'No. He refused to, in fact, no matter how many times I asked him. He said it was a private matter between him and you.'

'Can you describe him, please?' I quickly grabbed my phone, stopped it from recording and brought up a search engine.

'Oh, err. Well, he was about this tall.' She held up a hand to indicate his height at about six feet two inches. 'He had a beard, but not a full beard, more like a week of stubble, and he had huge hands. I remember seeing them and thinking about how big they were. Like gravedigger's shovels, they were. He had a nice suit though, so he couldn't have been all bad, nicely tailored and I think it was a wool blend, plus he was really muscular; he had no neck to speak of and I could see his biceps straining the fabric of his jacket when he moved so it had to be handmade.'

I held up my screen, showing her a picture of Ian Brevin. 'Was it this man?' she shook her head. I swiped to the next picture. 'This one?' she shook her head again. It wasn't either of the East End gangsters Charlie named. Which meant there was a third player who might have nothing to do with Maggie's murder. Or might even be the murderer himself come to make sure I didn't dig deep enough to find him. From her description, I was already certain I didn't want to meet him, but my brain was telling me I had missed something, something to do with this man in particular. There was something familiar about his description though I couldn't fathom what it was.

'So, what is the big secret?' Mavis asked, clearly desperate to know and feeling she had earned the right.

'I've opened my own detective agency,' I told her. I knew it wasn't the juicy sex scandal she was hoping for; Mavis loved a juicy sex scandal, but I also knew she would share anything she thought worth sharing, which at this point was the news that I had a business and my services could be hired. It was simpler, cheaper, and more reliable than putting an advert in the local paper. I could do that later as well, but this would get the word out for now. I wanted to work locally, not get drawn into cases that forced me to travel. I had to expect some mileage, it was inevitable, like the need to visit Maggie's office in London already. If I could get away with it though, I was going to focus on cases in my home county of Kent.

Mavis looked a little crestfallen. 'Is that it?' she asked. 'I was hoping you were going to tell me something exciting.'

'I think that is exciting, Mavis. I can't stay and chat any longer though, I have a case to solve, a police detective to meet and an office to inspect.' I waved goodbye and dashed out before she could pin me down for more detail, stopping at the front of the shop to quickly fill a basket with some essentials and paying the bored, and quite sullen-looking, teenager at the till.

Despite the news about the man with no neck asking people where he could find me, I was feeling good about my day and excited to get on with the next thing.

The next thing, I decided, was to look at the office in Rochester.

The Office

Rochester was classed as a city, with a castle and a cathedral and a rich history which included Charles Dickens living there for most of his adult life. It certainly had all the characteristics a city might expect to boast. I hadn't been there for years, there being nothing to draw me in that direction, but I was familiar with the road layout and found my way to where I wanted to be without needing to consider my route.

Mercifully, the car continued to behave, so it got a pat as I slid out of the driver's seat and paid for parking. The office, the owner assured me, was not far from North Gate, the ancient entrance to the city, and the Cathedral which sat behind it. This made it easy to find, as the Cathedral, even if one didn't know where it was, dominated the skyline.

Rochester is a busy area, tourists drawn from Europe finding it was easy to get to, but English tourists flooded there in numbers as well. With a lot of passing trade, the High Street, which ran for most of a mile, was filled with quaint little artisan sweet shops and bakeries and non-franchise restaurants. Tony Jarvis Travel, the little travel shop the office sat above, was a tired looking place that oddly seemed in keeping with the other buildings around it. The architecture of the surrounding buildings was Elizabethan, I thought. It was certainly many centuries old so a modern façade would look out of place and was probably prohibited by the town planners.

Tony told me I could drop by at any point during normal office hours and expect to find him there, except between one and two when he took lunch. It was still late morning, but I wasn't going directly to find him, I wanted to scope out the premises first without a hungry salesman jabbering in my ear.

Having parked in the large car park half way along the High Street, I was walking north toward the river, passing familiar shops still standing in the same place they had occupied for decades. Some of them even displayed established dates, the oldest I spotted was 1673. It seemed quite the feat though I doubted my little private investigation agency would last that long. I was sure I had read somewhere that most businesses fold in the first year. If they can get past that, they might go on for decades.

I was being determined but cautious with my approach, spending what I had to and making savings where I could. The office was one of the savings. Anna led me along the High Street, her determined pace dragging me along though she had no idea where she was going. Looking for it, I spotted the office about fifty yards before I got to it. It had a prominent position overlooking the High Street with a pair of windows looking down over the people outside. The website boasted as much but Tony had warned me it was rather small; just big enough for a desk and a small table to meet with clients. It sounded perfect.

As I neared it, I spotted something else and tugged at Anna's lead to stop her.

Twenty yards away from the office I wanted to rent, was the other investigation agency I found when I searched yesterday. The paranormal one. I stood facing the office and marvelled at how plush it was. Inside I could see a man and a woman moving about and another woman sitting at a desk a short way inside the door. Blue Moon Investigations were doing well for themselves, that was for certain. It buoyed my hopes for the market in general, so I pushed on to find Tony Jarvis inside his shop.

I was barely through the door when a man jumped up from a desk and began bounding across to me. He had to be in his late sixties and looked every year of it. His mousy, thinning ginger hair and a very pale complexion on a tiny frame reminded me of a weasel from *Who Framed Roger Rabbit*. Despite, all that, he was brimming with energy and bore a genuine smile of pleasure as he extended his hand to me. 'Mrs Fisher, yes? I recognise you from the television.'

Another one who knew who I was without me needing to introduce myself. I had to hope the notoriety would fade with time. 'Mr Jarvis?'

'Indeed. Owner and proprietor. You are interested in my spare office? It has just been fully refitted and there's a new roof so no chance of a leak in the winter and I got it double insulated so you won't get cold either, not that the last tenant ever complained about it being cold.' He started toward the door I had just come through, being careful to step over Anna as she sniffed his feet. 'Judy mind the shop, I'll just be a few minutes with Mrs Fisher,' he shouted as he pushed the door open. Judy didn't even look up from the magazine she was reading.

Outside, he walked back the way I had come, ducked through a gap in the wall that led to a carpark and arrived at a door on the side of his building. 'You can park here all day for free,' he said, pointing to two parking spots marked out on the floor. The line paint was fresh.

'What happened to the last person to rent it? Why did they leave?'

'Ah, well, yes, that's something of a story actually. The last chap was something of a sleuth too, but he attracted some unwanted attention from the people he investigated every now and then. One particular occasion last year, right around Hallowe'en it was, some of them set fire to his office with him in it.'

'Oh, my goodness,' I gasped. 'Did he live?'

'Oh, yes,' Tony chuckled. 'He's a hard one to kill that Tempest Michaels. You might have heard about it actually, there was a huge fight at the castle between two opposing gangs of clowns.'

I had heard about it. It was all over the national news at the time, but it was the man's name that was stuck in my head now. 'Tempest Michaels. That's the Blue Moon guy, isn't it?'

'It certainly is,' Tony confirmed. 'Well, the office went up in smoke and flame so I had it all rebuilt, paid for by the insurance thankfully, but he couldn't wait, and his business was growing so he moved to a vacant property just along the street.'

'Yes, I saw it,' I murmured. I was wondering what I was getting myself into. Solving mysteries onboard the Aurelia had been hairy and dangerous at times. I probably could have been killed by several different people on several different occasions and only survived some of them because people came to my rescue. I was all by myself now though, no back up to call on, no squad of ship's security to arrive with assault rifles, no ninja-trained butler. And I already had a musclebound man in a suit looking for me. Would I live out the first week? The annoying voice in my head told me I wouldn't need to worry about the divorce paperwork or finding a new place to live if I got myself killed now. I told it to shut up and wisely chose to not mention my life expectancy to Tony just in case he changed his mind about renting me the office.

Inside the door, a set of wooden stairs led up. They were brand new too and didn't creak or groan once as we ascended them. I had to scoop Anna and carry her up the stairs; her belly was just too big now.

'That's ironic,' Tony commented.

'What is?'

'The dog. You don't see many Dachshunds around, but the other fellow, Tempest, he had two.' Now I was really curious about him. I would have to introduce myself at some point.

At the top of the stairs was another door. This one had a large glass panel so I could see out at who was coming up the stairs before they got to me. I could also put a business name on with some frosted letters like an old-style gumshoe if I wanted to. Inside the space looked big. It was empty though, so I tried to imagine it with office furniture. In fact, I tried to do a mental tally of what office furniture I would need since, until that point, I hadn't once considered it.

Tony, who had been going hard sell since I met him five minutes ago, was now standing to one side and staying respectfully quiet while I looked about. I had to admit that I liked it. It had a real period feel to it; there was lots of wood left exposed but delicately shaped as a master craftsman would have done centuries ago.

When I turned to meet his eyes, Tony said, 'There's a small corridor just through this door,' he indicated like a game show host. 'It leads to a toilet and a storeroom which we can share. It's all included in the monthly rental figure.'

He was waiting patiently for some feedback from me. I shrugged and said, 'I'll take it. How soon can I move in?'

He looked relieved, like a starving man who had just been given a scrap of bread. 'I'm so pleased,' he announced exhaling and deflating as if he had been holding his breath for an hour. 'My wife has been nagging me to rent this place for months. I'll give you a key and you can move in as soon as you like. Everything should work but if you find a glitchy socket or anything at all, just let me know.'

We agreed on some details, I arranged a transfer of the first full month's rent as a deposit to get me started and I took a set of keys. All of a sudden, I had an office and a parking spot and a business account and a client with a case. Unfortunately, all that meant I now needed to buy or rent some office furniture, get a computer and teach myself to use it, sort out a domain name - whatever the heck that is. I had no idea, but I knew I needed one if my business was going to have a website and I was certain I couldn't go without in the 21st century. There was a stack of things to do but top of the priority list was to solve Maggie's murder. That would earn me money and I needed money to pay for all the things I needed just to get this idea off the ground.

I thanked Tony and left him in his shop just as free of customers as it had been when I arrived. The next item on my list was to meet with DS Atwell if he could fit me in. It was already later than the late morning rendezvous he suggested, but I didn't get the impression he would mind or that he was very busy. I paused in the High Street to call him.

He answered on the third ring, 'Detective Sergeant Atwell.'

'Detective Sergeant Atwell, it's Patricia Fisher. I was hoping you might be able to make some time for me. Do you fancy some lunch in West Malling?'

'Well, well, this is my lucky day. Do you have a place in mind?'

'Gregor's Barn? I haven't been there for a long time, and it's a nice day so we can sit outside.' If my memory served me correctly, it was convenient for parking and served a lot of quite healthy dishes so I could select something Barbie would approve of. Thinking of my blonde friend caused a twinge of sadness. The Aurelia was due to sail tonight and all the friends I had made there would leave forever. 'Shall we say, one o'clock?'

'One o'clock it is,' he agreed. We said goodbye and the call ended just as I noticed a man being dragged across the pavement by a brace of black and tan Dachshunds. I hadn't seen where he had come from, but the dogs had spotted Anna and were determined to meet her.

He did his best to reign them in, pulling them back until they were on a short lead but letting them get to her anyway. He glanced up to meet my eyes before looking back down at the three dogs fussing about and sniffing each other. 'Hi. It's so rare to see another sausage, I think they got a little carried away. Your little girl looks fit to burst though.'

'Yes, I don't think it will be many more days before she delivers.'

Then he looked at me properly for the first time, just as I looked at him. 'Wait, you're Patricia Fisher. Hi, I'm...'

'Tempest Michaels,' I provided, making the logical jump using the information I already had about him coupled with the fact that we were standing five yards from his office.

'Yes,' he replied, unsure how I knew who he was but not questioning it.

Silence fell and stretched out for a second, the dogs and their madly whizzing tails taking our attention. I broke the quiet when I said, 'I should probably tell you that I have opened a rival investigation business. Not paranormal stuff though, just straight up vanilla cases, I'm afraid.'

He nodded in understanding. 'Thank you for letting me know. It seems likely we can help each other out though. I get clients whose cases are not our usual paranormal fare. I can pass them your way and perhaps you will get the odd weird case you might want to throw to us.'

'That sounds good,' I agreed.

'Where are you setting up office?' he asked.

I had to smile now, amusement catching the corners of my mouth. I pointed upwards, his eyes tracking my finger. 'I rented a little place from a chap called Tony Jarvis.'

Tempest broke into a broad grin too. 'Brilliant. We shall be neighbours. Well, nice to meet you. I hope we can catch up soon. Pop in for a coffee whenever you have a few minutes to spare. I have to go; Amanda and I are looking into a troll sighting.'

I laughed but then realised that he wasn't joking. 'Righto. Good luck,' I hailed after him as he slipped into his office. He was a thoroughly pleasant young man, which I then realised was the same *young* descriptor Mavis had used for all people under forty. Tempest had to be in his late thirties but he looked young and athletic, a bit like Jermaine in many ways in that he clearly looked after himself and Tony's comment about being hard to kill made me think he was probably able to handle himself.

There I was thinking about Jermaine again. I had to wonder how long it would be before the constant references to my friends on board would fade. It was a question that wasn't helped when my phone rang as soon as I started walking and I discovered it was Alistair calling. I almost didn't answer it; we had said our goodbyes last night in the sweetest way I could have imagined. It was a lovers' parting and it was done. We both had to accept that our paths lay along different lines, but perhaps he wanted something important.

'Alistair?' I asked, worried for what reason he might be calling.

'Hello, darling,' he replied, his deep, throaty growl making me instantly think of the bedroom.

'Alistair, what is it? Is someone in trouble?' I prayed that wouldn't be the case. If I had to return to the ship, I wasn't sure I could stand to leave it twice.

'No, dear. No, nothing like that. I just wanted to hear your voice. I wanted to appeal to you to change your mind. Come back to the Aurelia, Patricia. It is already feeling empty without you here.'

'I can't, Alistair.'

'I spoke with the cruise line and they have agreed to extend your stay in the Windsor Suite free of charge. You have brought them so much free publicity, you see.'

I could feel an irrational anger rising. We said our goodbyes last night, but now he was spoiling the memory. I missed him. I truly did; saying no to his invitation to sail the world as his lover was one of the hardest things I had ever done, but I truly believed it was the right choice. Not only that, I knew my biggest reason to stay on board wasn't Alistair but Jermaine and that was a relationship I could not hope to perpetuate because I couldn't afford to spend the rest of my life in a royal suite with a butler.

Softly, I said, 'I'm sorry, Alistair. I am not coming back. Not ever, I don't think. I have to ask that you respect that. Please call me, message me, send me an email, but don't ask me to come back when I cannot. I opened my own business yesterday and I already have a client.'

He was silent at the other end for a few seconds, before saying. 'I expected as much, Patricia. I hope you understand that I had to have one last go at stopping you from breaking my heart. If you ever change your mind, if you ever want to have a short getaway, I will fly you to wherever we are, and you can stay with me as my lover or just as my friend. I will be glad to see you whatever the reason.'

It was a better invitation than anyone deserved, and I thanked him and said goodbye. As I slipped the phone back in my bag, I couldn't help but feel alone. I didn't really have any friends, not close ones that I could easily get to. I had no lover, having rejected Alistair so he could stay with his ship, and I had no work colleagues. It was just me against the world and right now, at this precise point in time, I wanted more. A tear slipped from my eye.

How was I to know how ironic my wish would soon prove to be?

Lunch with DS Atwell

DS Atwell looked better today than he had last night. There was more colour in his face for a start. I found him sitting at a table for two in a sunspot. It was warm for early autumn as it so often is in the southeast corner of England, a healthy twenty centigrade or thereabouts; quite warm enough for a light lunch outside. He stood up as I got to the table, showing his manners but not over doing it by trying to get my chair. He was already nursing a half pint of stout but signalled a waiter to attend while I settled into my chair. I ordered ice-water, knowing Barbie would approve and that it was counterintuitive to have alcohol today when I got up to run this morning.

'How are you finding being back in England after your tour of the globe?' he asked to make conversation.

'I haven't yet found my feet, if that is what you are asking. I seem to have a fair bit on my plate, including a divorce to organise and I need to find somewhere to live.'

'Busy times. And on top of that you have a case to investigate.' The waiter returned with my water and we paused for a moment to peruse the menu and order food. DS Atwell chose fish and chips, which sounded delicious but also filled with far more calories than I could permit myself, so I selected a quinoa bowl which the menu bragged was less than five hundred calories. More than that, it was filled with all manner of easily digested whole grains and lots of roasted root vegetables. It would tick a lot of boxes even if guilty satisfaction wasn't one of them.

As the waiter departed, I got down to business. 'You have information for me? Do you mind if I record you?'

He chuckled, a few huffing breaths escaping him. 'Yes, I do mind. I'm about to undermine one of my superiors and give you information that I myself cannot use. It is sensitive and potentially dangerous to you. I would not give it to anyone normally, I can't say that I have done anything like this before ever, but it seems appropriate today because I think you can handle it. The local papers picked up on your story when the sapphire was found. Local girl makes good was the spin most of them put on it. That was months ago, and they followed you ever since so I got to read about the shootout with the rival gangs from Miami, and the thing with the Indian television crew, and the terrorists with the Ebola virus. That's how I know you can be trusted to see this through.'

'Right, no pressure then.' I made a joke of it, but it didn't feel like a joke at all.

'At the heart of this case are two very dangerous men.'

'Jim Brevin and Ian Drummond,' I supplied.

I got a raised eyebrow from him. Then he laughed, a deep belly laugh that got the attention of several other restaurant patrons. 'You're no slouch are you, Mrs Fisher? I don't know why I am acting surprised.'

'Please, call me Patricia.' I insisted.

'As long as you call me Mike.' With that settled he pressed on. 'I will tell you everything I know about the case, Patricia, which is mostly what I managed to work out before it was taken away from me. I expect though that you will already know most of it given how intuitive you seem to be.' He took a sip of his drink and settled slightly in his chair, getting into story mode. Then, with a wriggle of his lips and a pinch of his nose, he started talking. 'I was called to Mrs Jeffries house almost immediately after the call came into the station. Her body was found by her cleaner, a young woman called Emily Walker. Miss Walker has a key to the property so let herself in, as was her usual practice, and claims to have been cleaning for more than half an hour when she discovered the body. I thought it odd that she could be there and not bump into Mrs Jeffries, but she insisted that was not unusual. Mrs Jeffries, she claimed, was almost always in her office at the back of the house, or still in bed. According to Miss Walker, she only checked in the office because she needed to use the vacuum cleaner and wished to make sure her employer wasn't still asleep.

Miss Walker is self-employed and had worked for Mrs Jeffries for more than two years. The murder itself looked to be a professional hit. That was my first impression and one which lasted. There was no passion, you see. It was a single shot to her right temple, the killer coming up behind her or somehow catching her unaware.'

'Why do you say that?' I wished to clarify.

'Her desk faces the door at an oblique angle. A person could not get into the room without the person at the desk seeing them. My initial thought was that someone might have been hiding in the room waiting for her to arrive, but there were no hiding places. I then wondered if it might be possible to come in through a window, but this also seemed unlikely as they were all locked and I cannot imagine how they would get in without the person sensing them. Even a deaf person would notice the change in air pressure. Our killer was able to walk up to her and shoot her even though she knew they were in the room.'

'She knew they were there?'

'That is my belief,' he confirmed.

The waiter returned with our meals. My quinoa bowl screamed healthy but boring, however, I found it was filled with flavour and texture. Mike's piece of cod was big enough to hang off both sides of the plate, but he looked at mine with a tinge of jealousy. When I caught his eye staring at my bowl, he said, 'I know I am supposed to order the healthy option, but I always manage to talk myself out of it.'

'It's not easy to avoid the naughty stuff,' I agreed.

'Yet you managed it.'

I nodded. 'You were telling me about her killer being in the room with her. You think it was someone she knew.'

He finished chewing his first bite of fish and added more tartare sauce from the small ramekin they provided. 'This is where it gets interesting and how I came to lose the case.' Now interested, I paused my own fork to listen. 'Part of her security system is a camera above the front door. It records everyone who comes to the house on a one-week loop. We got excited when we found it because we expected it to show the killer arriving, but no one came or went from the house that entire night. It doesn't film the gardens or any other approaches unfortunately, or we might have already caught the killer, but it does show two very specific and well-known East End businessmen ringing her doorbell a few hours before her murder.'

'Jim Brevin and Ian Drummond.'

'That's right. They arrived at eight minutes after three in the afternoon, stayed for more than an hour and left again. Mrs Jeffries was killed somewhere between six and seven that evening. The surprising part about their visit is that they came alone, by which I mean they hadn't turned up with their usual full entourage of hoodlums and leg breakers. I am told they never leave London and never go anywhere without protection. These are dangerous men as I mentioned earlier. Suspected of running a good portion of London's drugs trade, prostitution, gambling, protection and money lending. My gut tells me it is the last of those that caused the murder.'

My brow furrowed. 'Money lending? But I thought she was rolling in money?'

'Yes and no,' he replied. 'There are some anomalies with the accounts.' I was going to kill Charlie this time. Why had he chosen to not mention what had to be an important factor?

'Such as?' I asked, mentally cracking my knuckles as I thought about throttling my husband.

'Some large sums of money going in and out of the accounts in the recent weeks. We had a forensic accountant go over it as a standard part of the investigation. Over the last year, the amounts fail to tally, but we haven't yet worked out why the books don't balance. Sums were going out but not coming back. It was mostly small stuff but always going out and always going to the same account. It was taken off my hands before I got to find out who owned the account in question. Every time it was labelled as marketing expenses which seems to be a catch-all for bits and pieces of petty cash but not the sort of sums we were seeing. It was three thousand here and then five thousand there. In total it was close to one hundred grand. Then recently a sudden injection of cash brought the books right back to square. A day later, most of that sum vanishes again. Less than a week after that, Mrs Jeffries has two gangsters visit her house and two hours after they leave, she is murdered in what looks like a professional execution.'

'Who had access to the accounts?'

'Only three people. They have an outsourced accountancy firm who does their books once a year. That is due shortly which might explain why the money went back in recently but not why it then went out again. Otherwise, the three people are Mrs Jeffries, Mathew Hughes, the firm's manager, and...'

'Charlie Fisher,' I finished his sentence for him.

'That's right,' he agreed.

'What do you know about your husband's dealings with Mrs Jeffries business?'

Anger clouded my expression. 'Nothing until last night when I found his name on a Companies House document in her bedside table. He kept that hidden from me for years.' Mike made an oops face. 'Did you talk to Brevin and Drummond?'

He flipped his eyebrows and smiled wryly. 'That's where it got away from me. Chief Inspector Quinn got wind that there might be an organised crime element to the case and whipped it out from under me. He is very career orientated so I expect he used the information to grease a wheel somewhere.'

'How do you mean?'

'He handed it off to the organised crime unit but will have done that to ingratiate himself or to win favour. He could be a good cop, but he is only interested in getting to where he wants to go. For him, that is all the way to the top. He might do it too.'

'You were told to drop the case?'

'Essentially, yes. It was being handed over to a branch that specialises in such things. They took all my notes, all the camera footage and other evidence; everything we took from her house is now with them. Not only that, I was required to report any new developments as the man on the ground.'

'Have there been any?' I asked.

He snorted. 'Only one.' He paused to make eye contact. 'Someone broke into her house last night and tripped the alarm.' I felt my face colour. 'Other than that, there has been nothing.'

Pushing my embarrassment down, I asked, 'Isn't it odd for the two top men to turn up in person?'

'I thought so too, but I never got the chance to find out why. My best guess is that she was siphoning off money to use for something and put it back at the last moment by borrowing from the Old City Firm. Quite why she would do that, I cannot fathom. But let's assume she did and then wasn't able to pay it back.'

The dates didn't add up for me. 'How long would they give her to return the loan? If she only borrowed it a week ago, surely they wouldn't have killed her already.'

He shrugged. 'Maybe she told them she wasn't going to pay it back. Maybe they knew she couldn't. Perhaps it was something else. Like I said; I got taken off the case before I really got started. Add up the facts we do know though and you have a professional hit with two known gangsters on the scene two hours before her death and no other suspects.'

It felt sloppy to me. I couldn't work out why two men with a gang of henchmen at their disposal would expose themselves like that? Choosing to come in person had to have a really good reason behind it. Exploring what it was felt genuinely dangerous, but I couldn't allow that to put me off.

'What about the office manager, Mathew Hughes?' I asked. 'Charlie said he has been away from the office for two weeks and no one can get hold of him.'

'Yes.' Mike skewed his lips to one side. 'I was looking into him when I got taken off the case. Primarily this is a murder investigation and he disappeared several days before Mrs Jeffries was killed. I marked him as unlikely on my suspects list and when I looked into him, his parents claimed he had gone on an impromptu holiday. He told them Mrs Jeffries arranged it as a reward for all his hard work. His fiancée was supposed to be going with him and he told his parents he was going to Bali. I didn't get far enough to check whether he did or not though.'

I ran it through in my head. 'There are three people who could be fiddling with the books. One is my husband and I don't think he would stoop that low; he's too much of a weasel to break the law, he'd be too worried about getting caught. One is dead and the other has suddenly absconded.'

Mike agreed with my line of thought. 'Murder is almost always caused by sex or money. Sometimes both.'

'Then I need to find Mathew Hughes,' I murmured more to myself than anyone else. Anna heard my fork scrape the bottom of my bowl and pawed at my foot. There was a small amount of the healthy, tasty quinoa left and I had eaten my fill so I checked around to see if there might be any disapproving wait staff watching and placed it on the floor for her to finish. She made short work of it, vacuuming up the last few morsels to leave a plate that could go straight back in the cupboard without touching the dishwasher.

Lunch was done, I had picked DS Atwell's brain, and I needed to get moving. I didn't want to take Anna to London with me though, so I was going to drop her off at Mrs Crawford's. I shook Mike's hand, paid for the meal, and thanked him for his time.

He stood up to see me off, saying, 'I expect our paths will cross again soon enough, but please call me anytime you have a question. There's so little that happens out here in the countryside, it would be nice if you could bring some action with you.'

I smiled at the thought and prayed it wouldn't come true, but I said, 'I'll see what I can do.'

Then I left him and walked back to my car, little Anna waddling as she pulled me along the street. Not for the first time in recent weeks, my brain was whirling with dozens of pieces of information, none of which I could fit together yet. There were connections here somewhere, I just couldn't see what they were, and I felt a little overwhelmed from it.

Heading back to the bed and breakfast to drop Anna off, a little bit of intuition mixed with some heathy caution made me do a drive by. It was a good thing I did because it probably saved my life. Standing at Mrs Crawford's door was a large man wearing a suit, the kind of man that appears to have no neck and was just as broad and dangerous looking as Mavis described him. Not only that, I now knew where I had seen him before. He had been waiting for me outside the Aurelia. He looked like a contract killer, the kind of man who might decide to kill a person with a thumb or perhaps a tiddlywink just because he hadn't used that method in the last few weeks. I wasn't going back to Mrs Crawford's any time soon.

So where could I go?

It didn't matter too much, I thought. The more obscure the better, so where would they never think to look for me? Instantly I thought of Maggie's house, but I would just trip the alarm again, plus I didn't think I would be able to sleep where her murder had so recently taken place.

Let's assume that he had done some research into me. If he had done some but not much, then the first place he would have looked is my home address where they would have met Charlie. It was that, I considered, or he would have really done his homework, in which case he would know we were separated and wouldn't bother checking at Charlie's.

I couldn't say it pleased me, but I was going home.

Charlie's House

'Have you solved it already?' Charlie asked as he opened the door.

Anna was doing her usual thing of straining at her lead to get inside. It was a house and that meant couches to sleep on and the very real possibility of food. Less than half an hour ago, I had given her a few spoonsful of the quinoa bowl when I couldn't finish it all, yet she was already looking for her next snack. It wasn't a pregnancy thing, it was a dog thing; she, like most of her kind, was permanently hungry.

'No, Charlie,' I scoffed. 'Not yet.' I had only been off the ship a little more than twenty-four hours. 'There's a person looking for me. I need a place to crash for a night or so.'

'What sort of person?' he asked, his eyes narrowing in concern.

I gritted my teeth as I wondered if I was going to have to ask nicely, something I wasn't sure I could lower myself to. 'The sort of person I would rather avoid. He is tall and muscular with no neck and he wears a very nice suit. He also drives a Jaguar, so if anyone turns up here looking for me that fits that description, don't let him in.' I accidentally on purpose let go of Anna's lead and she dashed over the threshold and into the house. Charlie spun around to see her whizz past and I used the distraction to slip around him.

Putting a hand on his shoulder to move him a foot to his left, I grabbed the edge of the door. 'Quick, shut it,' I insisted quietly, then abandoned him to look confused and surprised as I went to find my dog.

'Hold on a minute,' he called after me.

Now didn't seem like the time to get into a discussion, so I skipped that part. 'Thank you for this, Charlie. I promise to be out of your hair as soon as I can. I'll crash in one of the spare bedrooms.' There were several to choose from and none had ever really been used in the three decades we had lived here. An occasional elderly relative had visited years ago but most of them were dead now. They should have been filled with children but... well, there's not much point dwelling on that now. 'Don't worry, I'm going straight back out. I need to get to Maggie's office.' I was only going for completeness. I needed to see it and meet a couple of her staff. It would give me a picture of the business; the dynamics and relationships and I could ask there about Mathew Hughes. If there was a rumour about him sleeping with Maggie, I couldn't allow myself to trust it, but if the staff believed it, the likelihood that it was true would increase.

Charlie followed me through to the living room where Anna had indeed found a comfy spot on a couch. Tugging at the cushions and a throw rug folded neatly and balanced on an arm, she was nesting again, making a spot to have her puppies. That was when I realised I had yet to take her to a vet. The Aurelia had doctors on board but no veterinarian; very few people took their pets on board.

I knew where there was one, so vowed to tackle that when I got home later; they would have evening surgeries. Now wasn't the time for that; I was on the scent and I had another question for Charlie. Or perhaps that should be another accusation.

Wheeling around to look him straight in the face, I asked, 'Why didn't you tell me about the recent anomalies in Maggie's business accounts?' His lips flapped a few times as he tried to think of a lie. I had to wonder why I had never noticed how often he did this when we were together. I guess I was happy to live with the lies back then, swallowing it down to keep the peace. That wasn't happening any longer; today the question was followed up by a poke in the chest as I took a threatening step forward. He took a step back as my finger hit his breastbone. 'Don't bother with any excuses, Charlie. What did you do with the money?'

I was convinced that accusing him of taking it would drive the truth from him as he sought to convince me of his innocence. So, the answer I received came as a complete surprise. 'I needed it,' he blurted.

For a second I thought I must have misheard him. 'You needed it?' I repeated. 'Needed it for what?'

'To pay the damned bills, Patricia,' he snapped. 'You emptied the bank accounts, or had you forgotten that? Having money does not mean I have cash and there were outstanding bills to pay.' He stormed away a couple of paces, angry at himself or at me; I couldn't tell which but when he turned, he looked apologetic. 'Most of the money I have is tied up in investments. I can't easily get to it and were I to withdraw it suddenly before it reached maturity, I would lose most of the value it had accrued. Taking a short-term loan was the obvious answer and I knew Maggie paid almost no attention to her books anymore. That was why I phoned Mathew Hughes. I wanted to tell him I was temporarily withdrawing a lump sum and would pay it back in due course. I couldn't get hold of him though, so I took it anyway.' He looked at me and misread my expression as accusatory. 'It's not stealing, Patricia. It's not embezzlement. It's my money.'

'How much?' I asked. He mumbled something I didn't hear. 'Sorry, I didn't catch that.' He mumbled again, saw my narrowed eyes and hands balled on my hips and let his shoulder slump in defeat. 'A hundred grand.'

My eyes couldn't have gone wider if I tried. 'A hundred thousand pounds. What the heck did you need a hundred thousand pounds for?'

'What did *you* need a hundred thousand for?' he shot back 'That's how much you took when you ran away to sea. Near as dammit anyway. I had loans to consolidate, investments to make and,' he mumbled something else. I didn't bother asking him to repeat himself, I kept my fists on my hips and tapped my foot. He slumped in defeat again. 'Okay, fine. I was paying legal fees to a solicitor. They don't come cheap, you know.'

My eyes were squinting now and my forehead creased as I ran his words through my head. A light pinged on at the back of my skull as the clues lined up. 'Oh, my God. You were trying to wriggle out of giving me a fair divorce settlement, weren't you? You were secretly spending money on some high-flying legal firm to get you out of having to share your investments.' I could see the truth of it in his shame-filled and disappointed face. He was busted and his biggest regret was that I was going to get my hands on what he considered to be his money. Looking back, he had been a terrible husband, always giving me the weaker share of everything. I was supposed to be his queen, his princess, the one who filled his heart with joy, yet he drove a new Bentley with a six-figure price tag, and I drove a second-hand Ford worth less than a grand.

If there was any justice in the world, he would be forced to live in a cardboard box and beg for scraps. I blew my top. 'Charlie Fisher, this is just about the last straw. You are going to give me half whether you like it or not. I expect you to make a list of all the assets you have hidden from me and I want to see it when I get home. If I think for one minute that you are still keeping things from me, I will hire a solicitor who will leave you with nothing. Are we clear?'

'Crystal,' he stuttered.

'I'm staying here tonight. I need a place to crash for a couple of days but don't think I am any happier about it than you are.' Then I heard someone moving about. They were coming down the stairs. 'Do you have someone here?' I demanded to know. It was an automatic reaction but one I had no right to make. 'I'm sorry,' I said quickly. 'I have no right to ask that question. This is your house now and we are very much separated.'

He shot me a dismissive look. 'You don't need to get excited either way, Patricia. It's just the cleaner, Emily.'

The young woman appeared in the doorway of the living room. She had headphones strapped to her head, the type that fit right over the ear and drown out all outside noise. They came with no wires now, the sound system and all the gubbins it required connecting directly to the internet somehow. It was all a bit space-aged for me. I like a piece of vinyl.

She paused as if surprised to see me here but she knew who I was; we had seen each other many times in the past, mostly when she was cleaning Maggie's house, but she lived somewhere nearby because I often saw her at the post office or just out and about. Her car had to be outside, but I hadn't noticed it when I arrived.

'I'm all done for the day, Charlie,' she announced as she slid the earphones backward, letting them fall to rest around her neck. Then she turned her eyes to me. 'Hello, Mrs Fisher. Back from your travels?'

'Yes. I'm just crashing here for a few days while I get myself sorted.' I said the words without thinking. Again, it was an automatic thing; I didn't want people to think I was moving back in with my cheating, lying, worthless husband. She didn't need to know that though and it was evident from her face that she didn't care less.

In response she said, 'I hear you are looking into Maggie's murder. Is that right?'

I nodded. 'I am.'

'Good. She was my best customer. I always got a great tip and a present at Christmas.' I was sure she made the comment for Charlie's ears and I silently wished her luck in getting more than a hearty handshake from him this coming holiday season. 'I think she liked that I never saw anything when I was at her house, even when there was plenty to see.'

'You mean like my husband sneaking in there for sex?' I asked. It was unfair of me; she owed no loyalty to me, so had no reason to let me know about his affair and would probably have been sacked by Maggie if she had.

She seemed to not even notice though, moving straight on to her next question. 'Do you think it was those gangsters the police are looking into?'

It was a good question and being asked it directly like that made me consider how I wanted to answer. Slowly I shook my head. 'No, I don't think it was.' Her face betrayed her surprise. 'The time of death doesn't correlate. Or so I have been told.' My brain was spinning fast now and had just supplied me with that fact. DS Atwell told me they left two hours before she was killed, so the coroner had determined time of death and they hadn't done it unless they went back there and snuck in. 'I have only just started looking into the case so I cannot claim to have made any conclusions yet. However, my gut tells me it will be someone more local.'

'That's not what the police said,' she argued.

'No,' I agreed. 'It's not what anyone is saying, which means the killer is probably feeling quite relaxed at the moment. I hope to spoil their day.'

'Why do you care anyway?' she asked. It sounded like an offensive question, challenging why I was bothering to involve myself. 'Didn't she steal your husband?'

I had to smile wryly as I formed the answer in my head. Charlie had wandered a few feet away and was pretending to inspect the books on his bookshelf while not very surreptitiously listening to our conversation. 'She did me a massive favour,' I told her with my smile broadening. 'I'll admit I didn't see it at the time, but I am much happier single again. That's no reason to look into the case, of course, but I have a client with an express wish that I find the culprit and that is what I intend to do.'

'What's your success rate?' she asked, now fishing car keys from the pocket of her jogging pants as an indication that she was about to leave.

I had to think before I answered, but could only conclude that it was, 'One hundred percent so far.'

She made an impressed face. 'And you think the killer is someone local.'

'I wouldn't want to be quoted on it, but it feels more likely than the East End gangsters. Like I said: I'm only just getting started.'

She took a step back toward the front door, raising her voice to shout, 'Goodbye, Charlie.' Then lowering it again to say, 'Nice taking to you.' Then she let herself out and I caught a glimpse of her car tucked against the hedge at the far edge of the front garden. I should have seen it when I arrived, but I guess my mind was focused on other things.

Charlie asked, 'Did you really need to have another dig at me, Patricia? Do you intend to tell everyone in the village that I was a lousy husband?'

'I doubt I shall have to, Charlie. You'll have been branded as a cheat already so that puts you to the top of the lousy husband list. Hard to climb back down from there. It's not like you can uncheat now. I have to go to London. While I'm out, kindly take care of my dog or I might decide to change my mind about signing that paperwork when I get back.'

Then I stormed from the house, slamming the door behind me magnanimously. Which would have worked a whole lot better if I hadn't left my handbag inside. At least when he answered the door, he had the decency to just hold out a hand with it in so I could take it and not get into another discussion.

I was off to London and I was going to crack this stupid case.

Maggie's Office

The run into London on the train took just over an hour if one included the time it took to park the car in West Malling station, buy a ticket and wait for the next train to arrive. Kent, and particularly the bit I live in, is prime commuter belt for people working in London who do not wish to pay the diabolically high prices properties in the city command. I once heard that Exeter in Devon, some two hundred miles from the capital, was getting an influx of commuters now because the rail link could get there in under two hours. Two hours each way sounded like a lot of time to be sat on a train, but I guess it suited some.

Our closeness in Kent meant that trains ran regularly so I waited only six minutes before a train arrived and then spent the time on board looking out the window and wondering how all the pieces of this puzzle went together. By the time we arrived at Victoria Station, I had a few working theories but none which I felt I could rely on and I had used my phone to look at rental properties in the East Malling area. Nothing was immediately available, and everything looked too expensive. Another issue was that I hoped I would only need to be in it for a few months but the minimum rental period I saw was six months and that was on a property way out of my price range. It was a pickle of a problem I could not yet see a way out of.

From Victoria Station I took the Underground, boarding the Circle Line to Embankment and walked to Trafalgar Square. I thought it a demonstration of her success that she could afford an office so close to the heart of London. One couldn't see the square from the office, and it was a small office, but she had several high talent clients that I knew of because she liked to drop names, so perhaps the costly real estate paid for itself.

I hadn't warned anyone at the office that I was coming but I was greeted with a professionally friendly smile when I knocked on the glass door. A young woman with a shock of red hair set ablaze by the deep green satin blouse she wore buzzed me inside and waited for me to introduce myself.

'Hello, my name is Patricia Fisher. I'm an old friend of...'

Her mouth dropped open, which caused me to pause as I wondered what was happening, but then she started squawking, 'Oh, my God! You're the lady on TV! The one who solves all the crimes and stopped that prince from being assassinated.'

'He was a Maharaja, but yes. I'm an old friend of Maggie Jeffries and I am looking into her death.'

The young woman was around the desk already and I thought for a moment she was going to ask for my autograph. Instead she whipped out her phone. 'My friends are never going to believe this. I need a selfie,' she gabbled. Before I could argue or protest, she had an arm around me and the camera pointing at our faces. The young woman, who couldn't have been older than twenty-five, was doing something weird with her head to make it stretch her neck and was holding the camera a foot above our heads so we both had to look up. 'This gets rid of wrinkles,' she explained, proving that I had much to learn about the world still.

'I need to ask some questions,' I told her as her thumbs twirled a quick dance across the keypad on her phone. Having taken a picture, she was now tweeting it or something.

'Gosh, I'm all flustered,' she said while fanning herself. 'It's not everyday a celebrity walks in.' Then she considered her statement. 'Well, actually, we do get quite a few, I suppose. Anyway, ask away. I'm Julie, by the way. I probably should have led with that.'

Finally remembering her manners, she then offered me coffee. I declined, saying, 'Are there other members of staff here? I need to ask questions about the business's cash flow and about Mathew Hughes.'

'Oh, Mathew, isn't here. He told us he was going to Bali one afternoon and then just left. It was a Tuesday. Who goes to Bali suddenly on a Tuesday?'

'Yes, I'm aware that he is away. Did he give you any indication when he expected to be back?'

She shook her head. 'No, not at all. It must be about two weeks already so he should be back soon.' If he is coming back at all, I thought. 'We should ask Graham. He's one of the literary agents. He might know more; I think the two of them go out together quite a bit.'

Graham was in an office with a window looking out into an alleyway which was much the same as having a brick wall instead of a window. I suppose one could at least attempt to regulate the temperature by opening and closing it. He was talking on the phone, so we waited patiently outside until he was finished. Graham Hicks was Senior Vice President of Talent according to the plaque on his desk. I placed his age as somewhere around forty though he was completely bald and clean shaven which gave his head a cue ball look from the back as he faced away from us to look out the window at the wall opposite. He wasn't wearing a suit, favouring a collared shirt and thin sweater instead.

He ended the call with a promise to make whatever deal they had been discussing happen and spun his chair around to find the two of us looking at him. 'Ladies?'

Next to me, Julie was vibrating with excitement. 'Graham, this is Patricia Fisher!' she gushed. He didn't look like he knew who that was which I ought to have been thankful for. However, now was a time when prior knowledge might speed things up. Julie sighed as if he was being dense. 'The lady that stopped the assassination in Zambezi.'

'Zangrabar,' I corrected her.

It seemed to ring a bell. 'What can I do for you?' he asked, leaning forward on his desk but not getting up to greet me.

I strode into his office uninvited. He had the air of someone too important and too busy to spare me the time I wanted so I chose to force his hand. 'I'm an old friend of Maggie's and married to Charlie Fisher, the other director and original investor in the firm. I am looking into her murder and I need some answers.' Talking money got his attention as I expected it would. He didn't need to know that I only found out about the investment in the last twenty-four hours or that I was divorcing Charlie.

He got quickly to his feet. 'Can you give us a minute, Julie?' he asked, essentially dismissing her.

'I need her too,' I insisted, 'and anyone else that is in the office today. I don't have the time to interview you all individually.'

'Interview?' he questioned. 'Are you in the police?' It was a flippant reply with a rhetorical question. I wondered if I was going to have to make him feel small in front of his colleagues.

I gave him my stern look. 'No. I'm a private investigator with a better track record than the police. Do you have something you don't want me to find out?'

His cheeks coloured as he began to bluster. 'No. No, goodness. What could I possibly have to hide?'

'Very well,' I slowly turned my eyes away from his. 'Do you have a meeting room we can use, Julie? How many staff are in today?'

'Just the two of us, Mrs Fisher. There's only four that work here. Bob Cartwright is at a bookfair in Doncaster and Mathew is in Bali.'

I tilted my head a little and looked at Graham's door again. 'It says Senior Vice President,' I pointed out. 'But you have no staff to lead?'

'Mrs Jeffries said it made us look like a bigger firm and allowed our clients to think they were getting dealt with by the firm's top people.' She was clever like that.

There was a chair by his desk, so I grabbed that, moved it to one side and sat on it. 'Have either of you ever heard of Jim Brevin or Ian Drummond?'

They were not standing together so it was difficult to see both faces at once, yet neither reacted in a way that I thought was covering a lie when they said, 'No.'

'How about the Old City Firm?'

'The gang?' Julie asked. 'I had an uncle who claimed to be part of that gang, but my mum said he was full of sh...'

'So, you know who they are,' I interrupted. 'Have you any reason to believe they have anything to do with the firm's dealings?'

Graham's eyes went wide. 'Good grief, no.' Then he gasped. 'Is that what happened to Mrs Jeffries? Was she mixed up with them?' Then he gasped again and snatched up his phone from the desk. 'Is Matt in trouble?' He was instantly trying to make a call. 'I haven't heard from him since he left.'

I waited patiently for the call to ring out and go to answer phone. Graham swore and instantly started to send a text message. I turned to

Julie. 'What about you, Julie? Have you had any contact with Mathew since he left?'

She looked at me like it was an odd question. 'No, none at all. I get on okay with him at work but would never message him socially.'

Graham swore again and put his phone down, then caught us both looking at him and apologised for his language. 'No answer,' he explained unnecessarily. 'I can't get his fiancée, Sophia, either.'

'Do you know her well?' I asked.

'Not really,' he replied. 'I don't have her number if that's what you're asking. I sent her some messages on social media but got no reply. It's odd actually.'

'In what way?'

'There's no update on her profile. If the two of them are in Bali she ought to be posting new pictures all the time. She does the rest of the time. I got un update last month because she was buying broccoli, so it's like...'

'Yes?' I prompted.

He looked up with a dread look on his face as he finished his sentence. 'It's like she died.'

Now Julie gasped. 'Oh, my God! Did they track them to Bali and kill them both? Are we next?'

'Why would we be next?' Graham wanted to know, derision dripping from his voice.

Julie rounded on him, anger driving her to retort quickly, 'They are picking off the firm's staff one at a time, Graham. Maybe you are next.'

'You're overreacting,' he replied, not sounding all that sure that he believed what he was saying.

'Really?' she snapped. 'Have you heard from Bob today?' A beat of silence passed as they stared at each other, then Graham snapped up his phone again and had it to his ear a second later.

Julie looked about ready to panic. I placed a hand on her shoulder. 'I don't think Mathew went to Bali and I don't think anyone will target you.'

'How do you know?' she wailed.

It was a good question but all I had was gut feeling. It felt wrong that someone was targeting the firm. My brain insisted this was about money and that somehow Mathew Hughes had involved the Old City Firm, whether deliberately or not, and that had caused Maggie's execution.

Graham saved me from answering her question by gasping with relief when a voice answered his latest call. 'Oh, thank God!' he said at twice normal volume. 'I swear I thought it was going to be the police answering because they found your body in a ditch.'

We could just about hear the voice at the other end say, 'Why would I be dead in a ditch?'

'Because we are all being murdered by a gang of East End criminals. You have to get back here so we can come up with a plan, find out what they want and escape with our lives!' Graham had bought into the concept that they were being targeted in a big way. He was almost hyperventilating, when he answered Bob's next question. 'Mathew is dead, Bob! They tracked him to Bali and killed him there.'

I tried to get his attention to calm him down or interrupt before he made Bob drive back from Doncaster so terrified of being followed that he crashed his car because he was looking out for hit men.

He ended his call with, 'Just get back here!' and sagged onto the desk. 'I've got a wife and kids,' he wailed. 'I haven't done anything wrong.'

It took about fifteen minutes, but I eventually managed to calm him down while Julie made tea and found some biscuits; the sugar would help with the self-induced shock. Now that he was calm, and we were all sitting down, I went back to asking questions. 'What do you know about the firm's financial situation?'

Graham looked up from dunking his biscuit in his tea. 'What? Is the firm in trouble financially as well?' He failed to pay attention to his biscuit soak speed so as he attempted to lift it to his mouth seventy percent of if broke off and tumbled into the liquid. He said yet another bad word.

Patiently I replied. 'That's not what I said, Graham. I asked if you knew anything about the firm's financial situation. So far as I know the firm is doing very well but there have been some anomalies with the bookkeeping recently.'

He gave me a sideways look as if I was now accusing him of something. 'What sort of anomalies?'

'Money going in and out when it shouldn't have been.' I knew Charlie had taken a lump out recently, but DS Atwell said the instances of money going out went back many months. 'Amounts have been going out under marketing expenses for months.'

Graham shook his head perplexed, looking to Julie as if she might know something about it. I watched their eyes; neither had any idea.

'One last question: What do you know about Mathew's relationship with Mrs Jeffries?' I wanted to ask outright if they thought he was sleeping with her, but I worried I might be doing him an injustice if he wasn't. He could be completely innocent of any involvement in any of the odd things going on.

Julie made a face as she considered the question. 'I think they got on really well.' She looked to Graham to disagree with her.

He said, 'Yeah. I guess. She rarely comes here anymore. Mathew visits her once a week for a strategy meeting. I think that's just what they call it and it's probably more of a catch up with how the business is going.'

I had my answer. Sort of, anyway. He was going to her place once a week. It might not be for sex but, knowing Maggie, it almost certainly was.

I left the office shortly afterwards, accepting that there was nothing left to learn at this time. I genuinely didn't think they were in any danger but left them my number in case they thought of anything. Graham gave me Mathew's number and his home address and his parents' address. They were retired, which was about all Graham knew about them. He met them once he said but whether I could catch them at home or they would know anything more than he did, he couldn't say.

There was one final snippet of information as I got to the door. I asked him about Mathew's fiancée, Sophia. He didn't have her number or know her parent's address, but he did say that she came from money. Her uncle was an inventor. Someone who was involved in supplying the market with the first home computers back in the very early eighties. I hadn't heard of him, but the family made millions from it and she had been used to a luxurious lifestyle. I logged it in my head and wondered if it might prove to be important later given my impression that this was all about money.

Outside in the street, I fished in my handbag for a mint, looked along the street in both directions for a coffee shop where I could get a drink to go and was about to set off when both my arms were grabbed from behind.

Organised Crime

Each bicep was being held in a tight grip as two men appeared, one either side of me, to lift me from my feet and propel me forward to the kerb where a car waited. A third man, one I had seen but paid no attention to, was waiting at the car. He nodded and smiled at me, which seemed utterly incongruous given my situation, then opened the door for the men to stuff me inside. In less than two seconds I was in the car, my surprise still registering.

This is the point where I probably ought to be screaming and trying to escape, and I find it sad that I know from experience to not bother wasting my breath.

'Good afternoon, Mrs Fisher,' said the man in the front passenger seat. I was wedged in the middle of the back seat between the two men who grabbed me; the one who held the door had been left in the street, either superfluous to future events or perhaps following in another car with yet more hoodlums.

'Oh, yes. A lovely afternoon,' I agreed flippantly. 'Is there a particularly good reason why you wish to kidnap me today?'

'Kidnap?' the man echoed, managing to make his tone horrified. 'We haven't kidnapped you, Mrs Fisher. We just need to have a friendly word.'

'Then you should have started by being friendly,' I snapped. 'Bundling ladies into cars is generally deemed to be criminal behaviour, though since you are criminals, I guess I shouldn't expect any different.'

In the front seat, the only man to have spoken so far was fiddling with his coat and I sucked in a breath of terror as I realised he was trying to pull out a gun. 'I think there's been some misunderstanding,' he said as he finally pulled his hand clear. It wasn't a gun he was holding though, but a small wallet looking thing. He held it up and flipped it open to show me his police identification. 'We're the good guys, Mrs Fisher.'

Involuntarily, I made a choking sound of disbelief. 'Well, you could have fooled me.' I was angry suddenly. If I didn't already have enough people menacing me and threatening me, now the British police were joining in. 'If you're the good guys, perhaps you can prove it by letting me out here.'

'Ooh, no can do, I'm afraid. The gov'nor wants a word, you see.'

'I am being kidnapped then?'

'Not strictly, Mrs Fisher. Not strictly. If you would prefer it, I can have one of the boys place you under arrest.'

I couldn't believe what I was hearing. Now he was threatening to incarcerate me for not cooperating. 'On what charge?' I demanded.

'Ooh, I think obstruction of justice would stick. That would stick, wouldn't it, boys?' he got a chorus of agreement from everyone else in the car and I felt like swinging my handbag at a few of their faces, just to get some respect. They were treating this like it was all a big joke.

Before I could scream in rage and demand to be set free, the driver announced, 'We're 'ere, boss.' He turned the wheel to take the car up a ramp and across the pavement. He was heading into an industrial unit and a roller door which magically opened as we neared it. In three seconds, I would be inside a building and out of sight of anyone who could do anything about me being taken. Those three seconds went by too quickly for me to be able to react.

The boss in the front seat bumped the driver lightly on his arm with a fist. 'Get us a cup of tea, won't you, Errol?'

'Yes, boss,' he replied, getting out and walking away. The men sat either side of me hadn't moved yet and I wondered why until men approached from either side to open the rear doors. They didn't open from the inside; a great precaution if one likes to kidnap people.

Angrily sliding across the leather seat to get out, I spotted the boss and shouted to him. 'Hey!' He turned around. 'If your governor wants a word, he better get on with it. I have no patience for all this messing about so you will be forced to arrest me shortly.' It was an ultimatum delivered with a non-specific threat as I didn't say what would happen when my patience ran out. In truth, I would probably decide to just be more patient since I was surrounded by burly men with neck tattoos that might or might not actually be police officers.

'Yes, Mrs Fisher. I'll get right on that. Why don't you take a seat? Errol's just making some tea, how do you like it?'

I narrowed my eyes at him, wanting to fire a rebuke in return but deciding I was thirsty, and a cup of tea sounded good. 'White, no sugar, thank you.'

'Jolly good,' he replied. 'Errol?'

From somewhere across the room, Errol replied, 'On it, boss.'

I was inside an industrial unit, the high walls and high ceiling filled with exposed gubbins. Cable, air-conditioning ductwork, and pipes were all visible because it was cheaper for the builders to leave them exposed and no one cared if an industrial unit was pretty. The floor was concrete and would be cold in the winter. To one side a pair of panel vans, the type criminals would use for a bank robbery, were parked. The Mercedes we arrived in was currently abandoned in the middle of the room and another one; same colour, same model, was parked neatly adjacent to the roller door we came in through.

With nothing better to do, and with no one supervising me, I walked across to a portacabin office and peered through the window. Inside was a man bent over a radio set. In fact, now I looked about, the whole room was filled with electronic paraphernalia. There were maps on the walls marked with pins and ink circles and bits of string. There were pictures on the wall, and I recognised Brevin and Drummond among the line-up of unpleasant looking mug shots. I really was with the police, I concluded.

'Come away, please, Mrs Fisher.' It was the boss from the car again. He was standing behind me and indicating for me to move away to a table and chairs Errol had just finished setting up. He had even found a gingham tablecloth and was currently setting out a pot of tea with appropriate accompanying crockery.

When I chose to do as asked, he appeared to breathe a sigh of relief. 'I apologise for the subterfuge and rather undignified manner in which we brought you here, Mrs Fisher. I am head of the Metropolitan Unit on organised crime. My name is Superintendent James Jenkins. My entire team and I are posing as a rival gang to the established Old City Firm in a bid to draw their attention. Outside of these walls, it is imperative that the team stay in character, which is why we had to be seen to act as hoodlums when we grabbed you. You are unhurt?' he sounded concerned, his tone and mannerisms making me want to forgive him.

He indicated toward one of the seats as Errol began to pour the tea. 'Yes, thank you,' I replied, accepting that to take umbrage would be counterproductive. 'Your team is trying to catch the Old City Firm?'

'Among other organised crime gangs, yes. It is a slow process because the ones we want are not the ones visibly or physically committing the crimes.'

'You're talking about the men at the top, Brevin and Drummond?'

He nodded as if appreciating that he wasn't going to have to explain everything. 'That's right. They both did time decades ago when they were coming up through the ranks, but they got too savvy to be caught again. Now they operate as if they are legitimate businessmen, pretending to be respectable while ordering murders, running drug rings and operating half the capital's prostitution. That's why the murder of Mrs Margaret Jeffries is so interesting. They were there. We can place them at the scene of the crime just an hour or so before it happened. We haven't worked out why yet or what their connection to her is, but this is the best lead in years, and we might be able to take out two of the biggest players in London. Without them at the helm, the rest of the gang will collapse, and we can mop up the pieces.'

'Okay,' I replied, accepting everything he said but wondering when he was going to get to the bit about why he thought it necessary to grab me off the streets today.

'I have undercover operatives deep inside the Old City Firm's organisation. Men that have been there for years now, putting their lives on hold so we can bring these scumbags down. I cannot allow you to jeopardise their safety by getting involved. Please tell me that you understand, Mrs Fisher.'

I stayed silent while I ran his words through my head. 'No,' I said, while slowly shaking my head, 'I don't understand. How will my investigation jeopardise what you are doing or the lives of men you have undercover in their organisation?'

Superintendent Jenkins sighed deeply. 'Your interference will distract the Old City Firm's operation. If they focus on you, they may act erratically. This will create a chaos situation. My men are going to find out why they killed her and once we have that information, we will swoop. I can't have any wild cards that could spoil my hand.'

'What if they didn't kill her?'

He gave me an incredulous look. 'Of course they killed her. They're East End gangsters and probably responsible for a hundred murders or more between them. Do you know how often they leave their territory?' He asked the question but didn't wait for me to answer. 'Never. That's how often. They never leave. Which means they had something so important to deal with that the two of them left London and went out into the countryside for the first time in years, and it was so sensitive they went without any of their lieutenants or henchmen. They killed her and we can place them at the scene of the crime. As soon as I know why and have an airtight case against them, they are mine.' He emphasised his point by holding up a fist and squeezing it tight.

'I thought the time of death didn't tally with their visit?'

'It doesn't,' he shrugged. 'But that means nothing. It is out by a couple of hours, but it is not an exact science.'

'Oh?' I tilted my head in question. He was wrong and he knew it. 'But it is a very close science. We both know that, so you know that they left at least two hours before she died...'

'Look,' he snapped, cutting me off rudely, 'they did it, alright? I don't have all the answers, but I also have neither the time nor the patience to explain police procedure to an interfering amateur who is threatening to undermine years of work. You will back away from this case, or I swear I will find a reason to lock you up.' He was raging now, his face changing colour as he failed to keep his frustration in check.

To further annoy him, I remained perfectly calm and showed not the slightest reaction to his outburst. 'Your plan is to pursue them whether they are guilty of this crime or not? Very well, Superintendent Jenkins, I wish you luck in achieving the prosecution you desire. Will there be anything else, you incompetent idiot?'

A burst of laughter escaped Errol's lips. He quickly stifled it, but my insult pushed Jenkins to the very edge. Just as he was about to retort, I leaned forward to calmly throw fuel on the fire. 'You cannot hold me, Superintendent, and you know it. Any trumped-up charge you attempt to levy will be quashed in hours by my team of lawyers who will then go on to expose your feeble attempt to silence me and end their day with a round of champagne after destroying your career. Any questions?'

Superintendent Jenkins was seething. However, when he spoke through gritted teeth, he said, 'Escort Mrs Fisher outside will you, Errol?'

'What then, boss?'

'Just show her out and shut the door.'

Errol hesitated. 'You don't want me to drop her back where we found her?'

'No, Errol. I am sure she can find her own way,' Jenkins hissed.

I needed to get up now, but I was so full of adrenalin that I wasn't sure my legs would support me. Threatening a senior police officer with a band of lawyers who existed only in my imagination had been a bold play, one which might have backfired and landed me in a holding cell for the night. I wasn't sure whether he could file a charge against me or not but had chosen to call his bluff and see what happened. It worked, but now my knees were knocking together, and I felt faint and a bit sick.

Errol took a step back and held an arm out to guide me to a door. 'If you please, Mrs.'

Forcing myself to give the superintendent one final glare, I used the table to get myself up and onto my feet. They held. As I started to walk away and turned my back on him, Jenkins decided to have one last word, 'I would be careful if I were you, Mrs Fisher. It's a dangerous world you are playing in now, not some fancy cruise ship. Anything could happen to a lady on her own. Know what I mean?' It was a barely concealed threat, one which intended to scare me even if he didn't mean it. It worked though; my core tightened as the very real horror of the people I was investigating forced its way to the front of my mind.

I didn't reply, or even show that I had heard him. Instead, I followed Errol to the door and outside into the sunshine. The door closed behind me and once again I found myself alone. Keeping my feet moving, I found the pavement and tried to orientate myself. The door was on a different side of the building to the roller door I arrived through, but I managed to find the front entrance again and started back the way we had come. I needed to find a ladies' room soon and I really wanted to find one in a coffee shop where I could relax for half an hour and let the adrenalin drain away over a strong... scrap that idea, I wanted to find a pub where I could relax for half an hour with an industrial strength gin and tonic. Or maybe two.

As I walked, I thought about my argument with the superintendent. There was something about the organised crime element that just didn't seem to work. It wasn't just that they left before she was killed; I doubted the men at the top often did their own dirty work so they would have sent someone back to the house to perform the execution. I liked the local angle better, just as I said to Emily back at Charlie's house. The local thing fit better with DS Atwell's belief that Maggie had to know her killer. That didn't rule out Mathew Hughes, I suddenly saw, unless he really was in Bali and had left before her murder.

Ten minutes and a mile and a bit later, I was back in a more civilised part of the capital where offices and houses predominated, and the industrial units were far behind me. There I spotted a likely looking building, which, as I drew closer, revealed that it was indeed a public house and went by the name of The Rose and Crown; a good old English pub name.

At the point where I was about to cross the street to get to it, three cars screeched to a stop in front of me. They blocked my path and I thought it was Superintendent Jenkins come for another round until the middle car's front passenger door opened and Jim Brevin stepped out onto the pavement.

I probably should have been terrified but perhaps I had simply run out of adrenalin because all I felt was annoyed. 'Can't you wait half an hour?' I snapped at him before he had a chance to speak.

My question confused him, his face fighting with several emotions before settling on nonplussed. 'Get in the car,' he growled. His voice was like a bag of gravel had learned to speak and his accent was thick cockney. Okay, technically it probably wasn't cockney though he might have been born within earshot of the Bow Bell, but it was that guttural, half the consonants missing, accent popularly referred to as cockney.

'What if I don't?' I asked. 'What if I go for a drink in that public house and use their facilities. You can come with me if you like?'

He turned to look at the other men who had joined him on the street. I was essentially surrounded, five men crowding me and all of them now wearing an amused smile crossed with a confused face. I wasn't showing them any fear and they couldn't work out what to make of it. Brevin was checking their faces to make sure he hadn't misheard me.

'I'll tell you what, Mrs Fisher,' he growled. 'If you will kindly get into the car as requested, I won't have any of my men stab you to death in an alleyway right now. Is that a fair deal?'

I wanted to present a counteroffer, but my knees had gone to jelly again because I was pretty sure, unlike the superintendent, that his threats were completely genuine. In fact, I said nothing at all because I was convinced my voice would come out as a croak, so I primly tucked my handbag close to my body and got into the car. Just like before, I found myself wedged in the middle of the backseat with a large man pressed in on either side.

Jim Brevin got in the front passenger seat, clipped his seat belt and pointed down the road. 'We're going to go for a nice little ride, Mrs Fisher. My colleague and I would like to have a quiet word with you in private.'

I really didn't like the sound of that, but as the car pulled away, I accepted that I had no choice, and if their intention was to kill me today, they probably wouldn't bother with the little word. I would find out soon enough.

The car passed the pub, my head turning to look at it with a tinge of disappointment; I had so nearly made it.

From the front seat, Brevin asked, 'What did Superintendent Jenkins want?' His question caught me by surprise because he knew who the superintendent was. Jenkins thought he was invisible to the crooks, or believed the crooks were fooled into thinking he was one of them; that was the role he was trying to play, except he wasn't fooling anyone it seemed. Turning to look at my face, Brevin said, 'You look surprised, Mrs Fisher. Did Jenkins tell you he has undercover operatives inside our organisation?' My stomach tightened in fear again. 'Oh, don't worry, we knew who they were the moment they showed up. We recruited them deliberately, in fact. This way we can feed them false information and be certain they will never be able to catch us. In contrast, that idiot Jenkins has two people on my payroll inside his own team. I know every move he makes. Life is so easy with him leading the operation against us. So, my question again, Mrs Fisher. What did he want?'

I found my voice. 'He told me to back off and stop looking into the murder of Maggie Jeffries.' It was a simple and honest answer, given because I suspected he already knew exactly what the superintendent wanted me for.

'I thought as much,' he replied. I got no more from him though, or from anyone else in the car as we continued on for another five minutes to our destination. Which turned out to be a pub, would you believe it?

The Fox and Hounds, another very traditional public house name, sat on the confluence of Epping Road and Wopham Street, two roads in what appeared to be an ugly, run-down terraced house area somewhere in the East End of London. There was litter in the streets and graffiti on the walls. Just behind where we parked the car was a gang of pre-teens beneath an iron railway bridge that spanned the street cutting right through the row of houses on both sides. The houses that abutted the bridge must rattle each time a train went by and the noise had to be unbearable. Despite my assumptions, the properties looked occupied.

Brevin opened his door and started to get out, peering into the back before standing up. 'You said something about a drink, I believe, Mrs Fisher. Name your poison.'

Surprised by the turn of events, I figured a gin and tonic wouldn't do me any harm if they were about to kill me and would help to steady my nerves if they weren't. 'Thank you, I'll have a gin and tonic, please.'

He nodded and climbed out into the road. 'G&T for the lady, Dave. In fact, make that two; I quite fancy one myself.' The men to my left and right both exited the car, the one to my right then offering his hand to help me out. This was not what I expected. The driver, apparently called Dave, nodded in acknowledgement and went inside.

Everyone was going into the pub, but no one was trying to usher me along, as if my compliance was assumed. To be fair, running away now wouldn't get me very far and I had no idea how to get to a safe place if I tried. Plus, if they weren't going to kill me, I might as well get this over with. Mentally shrugging, I went through the pub door to find myself inside a stereotypical public house. It wasn't a big place but had separate saloon and lounge bars, wooden floorboards that might have been down for a hundred and fifty years and must have some tales to tell, and a brass foot rest running all the way along the front of the bar at ankle height. The décor was ancient dark wood panels with cream painted walls above from about head height up to the double height ceiling. Glasses hung above the bar and the forty-something barmaid wore a ton of makeup and a low-cut top to show off a seriously impressive amount of cleavage. It was as if they had gone looking for public house clichés and stuffed them all into one place.

I looked around for Brevin or anyone who might tell me where I was supposed to go now. Just then Dave appeared by my elbow bearing a tray on which he had three old and murky tumblers containing gin and tonic. 'Just through here if you please, Mrs Fisher,' he nodded with his head to a door in the corner.

He led the way, taking me through a door while balancing the tray on one hand and almost dropping it. A short hallway with a patterned red carpet led to a door at the back. I got the impression the pub was their headquarters, made more likely when Dave opened a door to reveal a sizeable office inside with Brevin and Drummond sitting at separate desks. Each faced the door and there was a table which could seat six to the right. Dave put the tray down on it and retreated, closing the door as he went out.

'Hello,' I said, mostly to see if my voice would work. This wasn't my first gangster's lair, but it's not the sort of thing a person gets used to. 'You wanted a quiet word?'

'We didn't kill Maggie,' stated Brevin.

It was quite the opener. I waited to see what else they were going to say. Both men got up from the desks and crossed the room. Surprising me again, each extended a hand for me to shake and politely introduced themselves.

'Jim Brevin. Sorry about all the hard man act. It's necessary in front of the boys.'

'Ian Drummond. Take a seat won't you please, Mrs Fisher?'

Trying to stop my eyes from flaring, I sat down and took one of the drinks, and then tried to not down it in one as I wanted to. Using both hands to keep it steady and beginning to feel less like my life was in mortal danger, I asked, 'How can I help you, gentlemen?'

Jim Brevin spoke first, 'We would like you to find out who killed Maggie, please.' It was not the sort of request one made if you had in fact killed the person yourself. Unless of course, you were being very clever. 'No doubt Jenkins told you we killed her.'

'What were you doing at her house?' I asked.

Ian Drummond fielded the question, 'That is between her and us, Mrs Fisher, and no one else in the world needs to know.'

'That's not a lot to go on,' I replied.

'It's quite enough to go on since we didn't kill her,' Drummond argued. 'Jim and I have followed your exploits, haven't we, Jim?'

'Indeed, we have, Ian. Quite taken with it we were when we heard about the Miami firms coming a cropper at your hands.'

'When we learned you were looking into Maggie's murder, we thought; I bet that Mrs Fisher will be able to solve this faster than those idiots in uniform. Isn't that right, Jim?'

'Indeed, it is, Ian. Unfortunately, we also thought; I'll bet that clever Mrs Fisher will follow the obvious breadcrumbs and shine a spotlight on us before she realises that we are innocent of this particular crime, didn't we, Ian?'

'Quite correct, Jim. We were very concerned about it, weren't we Jim.'

'Quite concerned, Ian.'

'So, Jim and I decided that we ought to intervene. To... prevent wasted effort on your part, Mrs Fisher.' Listening to the two crime lords was like watching a well-rehearsed double act. They went back and forth continually, each one making a statement so the other could agree and then extend it.

'I'm here so my time won't be wasted?' I confirmed.

'Yes, Mrs Fisher,' Jim replied.

'By looking into your affairs?'

'That's correct, Mrs Fisher,' said Ian.

Seeing a way out, I said, 'Then I should thank you. Thank you, gentlemen. It was very kind of you to consider me.'

Both men narrowed their faces. 'I'm not sure she means that, Ian.'

'No, Jim. I find myself worried that she is trying to escape our company only to continue her investigation regardless of our polite request.'

Bother. I tried to convince them. 'Gentlemen, I had already considered that you were probably not the killers. Any interest I had in you was for background as I tried to work out what was going on in Maggie's life leading up to her murder.'

'You need to forget about our visit to her house, Mrs Fisher. It's nothing but a red herring, isn't it, Jim?'

'It most certainly is, Ian. You should forget all about it, Mrs Fisher.'

'You're not going to tell me why you were there?' I couldn't help myself; I was getting more curious by the minute.

'It is a private and unconnected matter between Maggie and the two of us, Mrs Fisher. Isn't that right, Ian?'

'Indeed, it is, Jim.'

I felt like we could go around and around like this for days and I really needed the restroom now. 'Gentlemen, I can see that you are both very serious individuals and I have no desire to get on the wrong side of you. If all you want is my assurance that I will stay away from shining a spotlight,' I used their term, 'on your operation, then you can have my word. It would help me to know what your relationship with Maggie is and why you chose to visit her, but I will just have to manage without knowing.'

This time, both men smiled, Ian nudging Jim with an elbow. 'See, Jim. I told you she would be reasonable.'

'You did, Ian. You absolutely did.'

'And you wanted to cut her into pieces for the fish in the Thames. You are such a silly sod, Jim.'

'I cannot raise an argument, Ian.' They were discussing my death as the alternative to doing as they asked as if it were an everyday activity. Perhaps for them it was.

'Is there anything else?' I asked tentatively.

Both men turned inwards to check with the other, exchanged a few quiet words and decided, 'No, Mrs Fisher. Can we drop you somewhere?'

I didn't want to get back in their car and get taken anywhere, but I certainly didn't want to find my own way out of wherever I was, so I kindly accepted and had them drop me back at Victoria Station.

Thanking Dave, the driver, as I got out and feeling like I ought to be tipping him, I stepped on the pavement and stood still for a few moments as I looked about to see who was going to nab me next. No one was paying me any attention though, so once I found it in myself to relax, I strolled into the station to check the time of the next train to West Malling, saw that I had twenty-three minutes, and went straight to the nearest pub. It was roughly fifteen yards away.

Waiting for my drink to be made, there was a singular thought I just couldn't shift: Brevin and Drummond knew Maggie. Every time they referred to her, they did so by her first name, and I got the impression from them that she was a friend or a long-time acquaintance. Then it hit me: one of them was a former lover. I rolled that idea around in my head all the way home on the train, the sun setting as we sped south.

I might have the lover part wrong. It could be that they knew her another way, but I couldn't shake the feeling that they had visited her as old friends that fateful day and their relationship was somehow a key factor in her death despite what they claimed. I had no desire to ever meet them again, but regardless of my promise to not look at what they might have been doing with her, I had a feeling there would be no option if I was going to solve this case.

Having so much to think about made the ride home seem swifter than the fifty-five minutes it took, the journey longer on the home leg because the train stopped relentlessly at every village on the line.

It was long after Anna's usual feeding time, something I had never worried about before because I had Jermaine to deal with it. Now, I imagined her stalking Charlie for the last two hours, grumping and huffing at him as he ignored her.

About two dozen people disembarked the train at West Malling station, most of them undoubtedly returning home after a long day at a job somewhere. All of them displayed their familiarity with the service by sitting in the carriage which stopped right by the bridge one needed to take to reach the car park. I was in one of the rear carriages and had to walk almost two hundred yards just to get to the bridge.

By the time I reached the car park, the last set of taillights was already on its way out, vanishing into the darkness as the trees swallowed it. The car park was more than half empty now, a vast contrast to what I found when I arrived and had to circle twice looking for a space. My car was right at the back, parked against the fence but I could walk directly to it now that most of the cars were gone.

My head was filled with thoughts of dinner and what I might get myself. I still wasn't organised and thought a takeaway might be in order, or perhaps going out for dinner with little Anna since she had been left for many hours now. Too busy working out what I wanted to eat, I failed to notice the car coming toward me. Its headlights were off, so it didn't illuminate me as it pointed in my direction and the driver floored the accelerator.

Startled by the noise of a racing engine, my nerves saved me. Later I would tell myself that it was the constant state of threat that made me dive over the bonnet of the nearest car without even looking to see if I was in danger. Had I hesitated and looked around, the car would have smashed into me and pinned me to the car I was walking by. Instead, it missed me by inches as I slid across the paintwork to crash to the tarmac on the other side. The car rocked as I went over it, shunted by the other car and throwing any chance I had of a graceful landing. I hit my head painfully, feeling a tug as the skin of my scalp bit into the tarmac and tore. The car had caught a glancing blow, careening off and then racing into the dark. From the ground I caught a brief glimpse as it passed under a streetlight and then it was gone. It was a grey something, but I was rubbish with car makes and models, a hole in my general knowledge I really ought to tackle. I heard its engine roaring through the trees as the driver powered away to escape.

Once again, I found myself filled with adrenalin. The danger was gone this time, the attempt on my life a failure mercifully. But who the heck had been at the wheel? I wanted to call the police, but I knew there was nothing to be gained by it. They could take a statement from me but what could I actually tell them other than someone in a car almost hit me. Chances are, they wouldn't even take it seriously. They would assume the driver's foot slipped.

I blew out a breath of tired resignation and picked myself up. There was a hole in my jacket, right on the elbow where I had crashed to the unforgiving ground. I patted my head where I hit the ground and my fingers came away with blood on them. It wasn't bleeding badly but would be sore for days and the blood would make my hair sticky.

Cursing my luck but acknowledging that I had triggered this by poking into Maggie's murder, I wondered if I had already met the killer or said something to someone which had then reached the killer's ears. I went around to inspect the damage to the car. It was a red Audi A4 and neither new nor old. The driver's door had a dent where the other car hit it and some paint had transferred. I turned on the light on my phone and took some pictures. The paint that had rubbed onto it did indeed look to be grey but in this light could be silver or maybe even a metallic cream. Grey wasn't a helpful colour either since there are so many shades to pick from. Grey is by its nature ambiguous since it couldn't manage to pick between white and black, choosing instead to dither in the middle.

The paint was about all I had though. Checking around to make sure nothing else was going to happen and no one else was going to jump out at me, I walked briskly to my car, got in and drove swiftly back to Charlie's house with my senses set to hyper-alert. Only once I was inside with the door shut behind me did I even begin to relax. The idea of a takeaway still sounded good, but I wasn't leaving the house again until the morning; not after the carpark incident I wasn't. I would eat a piece of stale bread or whatever Charlie agreed to let me have and I would hide in the house until tomorrow.

I asked the darkness outside if that tactic would make any difference.

The Dangers of Jogging

I didn't get a lot of sleep that night, lying awake for hours trying to work out who might have been driving the car and how they had known I would be there. The original feeling that this was all to do with money had been replaced by the belief that Maggie had involved herself, directly or indirectly, in organised crime. That idea, however, had been replaced by a belief that the case was more local and her murder more likely to be someone trying to cover up their infidelity or get revenge for her ruining yet another relationship. Maggie took a lot of lovers; I knew that much; it was practically a local legend now. So, how likely was It that more than one husband had been sucked into her lair? One theory was that Maggie had threatened to reveal an affair and the man involved had taken it upon himself to kill her? It sort of worked as a theory if that man then found out that I was investigating and figured he needed to kill me as well. The methods used, shot to the head and run over by a car, were very different, but that didn't mean it wasn't the same person. If they were local, then they would know I was investigating.

I turned over in bed for the umpteenth time, telling myself to stop fixating on the case and get some sleep. My eyes pinged open again though when I remembered the Aurelia. It had sailed earlier this evening, probably while I was on the train and that portion of my life was finished with no option to change my mind. Until the ship left Southampton, I could have easily driven back there and taken Alistair up on his offer. Now it was too late. Oh, sure, I could fly to its next destination and still be welcomed with open arms, but that couldn't be performed as part of a scared whim.

I wasn't going back, and I knew for certain that I would never see my friends on the Aurelia again.

Eventually, I slept.

In the morning, I forced myself from bed at six o'clock, the alarm on my phone waking me as planned because I was going for a run. Charlie was up at the same time, getting himself ready for work.

He stared at me with a very confused expression. 'You're going for a run?' he asked, taking in the gear I wore.

'Yes, it makes me feel invigorated.' I replied, stretching my neck and shoulders and working down my body before opening the door and setting off. I was actively fighting my desire to go back to bed. Sleep had been fitful when fatigue finally overwhelmed the alertness I felt, so I hadn't claimed more than a few hours. The last thing I wanted to do was go for a run.

The rhythm of my steps came as I claimed the first half mile. My breathing settled and I didn't have to tell myself that this was a good thing to do because I already knew that it was. The route I picked in my head was somewhere in the region of four miles, taking on a winding route through the village. Forty-five minutes after setting off, I was nearly back at Charlie's house so let my pace slow to a gentle jog and then to a fast walk. There was less than two hundred yards to go when my foot slipped on a wet leaf. I didn't fall, I just stumbled slightly, but as I did, I heard the sound of something going by my head at speed. A nanosecond later, the sound stopped abruptly when it hit a tree and my incredulous eyes saw the butt end of an arrow quivering. It was buried an inch or more into the trunk of the tree and I was staring at it with utter disbelief.

Mercifully, my brain kicked into survival mode in time to make me hug the floor just as a second arrow ripped over my head to strike the tree two inches from the first one.

Someone was trying to kill me!

I broke into a sprint, thankful my muscles were warm and happy to respond as I demanded more from them. Terrified of an arrow in the back, I bobbed and weaved as I ran, making my movements erratic since I couldn't outrun an arrow but might be able to dodge one. Glancing across the street and into the woods on the other side revealed nothing. The archer could be wearing camouflage clothing or might have already chosen to flee having missed me twice. I wasn't taking any chances though; I was going to run all the way home and then maybe get on a plane going to Mexico.

I slammed into the front door of Charlie's house, realised he had gone to work and I hadn't taken a key and fought a rising panic that my attacker was even now lining up the shot that would skewer me to the door like a prize for Charlie to find later. Would he be pleased that he no longer had to bother with a divorce or share his assets?

Probably.

Was there a key under the stone by the drainpipe still? I darted to check, came up triumphant but felt too terrified to go back to the front door now. Instead, I ran to the corner and peeked out, staying like that for fifteen minutes before I struck up the courage to use the key.

By then, my hands had stopped shaking so, once inside, I called the number I had for DS Atwell.

'Good morning, Patricia. To what do I owe the pleasure of this call?' he asked jovially.

In return I blurted at him, 'Someone just tried to kill me.'

I got only a moment of silence before his gears got up to speed. 'Where are you? Are you still in danger?'

Relief that someone was coming to my rescue flooded through me, causing me to slump against a wall and slide down it to sit on the floor. 'I'm in Charlie Fisher's house. The big detached place on Moon Pond Lane.'

'I know it,' he replied quickly. I could hear him moving. 'Are you safe there?'

'Yes. I mean, I think so.'

'Stay inside, stay out of sight and stay on the line. I'll be five minutes.' True to his word, he stayed on the line and kept talking to me the whole way, pausing only to use the radio in his car to call for uniformed support when I told him about the arrows. His journey took him less than five minutes, the siren audible in the quiet countryside long before he arrived with a slewing spray of gravel on the drive outside the front door. Joshua and Marvin arrived less than a minute later but by then we were making tea and I had told him about the incident at the train station last night and the man with no neck.

'He's been seen in the local area?' Joshua confirmed.

'Several times. Mavis told me he had been in the post office asking for me and I saw him outside Mrs Crawford's. That's why I am staying here.' Joshua was making notes. 'He was also waiting for me when my ship docked in Southampton.'

'He followed you here from there?' asked Mike. I hadn't mentioned that bit earlier.

I nodded. 'I'm pretty sure it's the same man, but I don't have any idea who he is.'

Mike wriggled his lips as he thought. 'That was before you took on the case, right?'

'Only sort of.' I explained that Charlie had contacted me more than a week and a half ago, probably right after the police had interviewed him and he got scared.

Mike asked, 'Who else knew?'

'No one. Except my butler and my gym instructor,' I corrected myself. 'They helped me do a little research, but I don't see how anyone here could have known. I thought it was the killer but why would he be waiting for me at the docks unless he knew I was taking on the case.' Then a thought occurred to me. 'Charlie might have told someone!'

'Can you ask him? Get him on the phone now?' Mike prompted.

I shook my head. 'He would just lie about it anyway.'

'Really? When it's this important?' Mike couldn't believe what I was telling him.

I laughed. 'Especially when it's this important. Charlie will go miles to avoid admitting he had done something wrong.'

'Then it could still be the killer that was waiting for you at the docks and followed you back here.'

I shrugged. 'I suppose. It could also be a hired hitman from one of the people I put away on my trip around the world.' Having made that bold statement, I then had to explain about some of the potential enemies I might have accrued. I talked while Mike and the uniforms followed me back to where the arrows hit the tree. There we found that the archer had already removed them, taking the evidence but unable to cover up the two fresh holes and the gouge marks required to get the arrow heads out.

It took only a few minutes of searching for Joshua to find where the archer had been standing. There was no evidence to be gathered though; too much leaf litter and undergrowth for there to be footprints and nothing left behind though they intended to perform a more convincing inspection with a team later.

'What about the car last night?' Mike asked. 'What can you tell us about it?'

I skewed my lips to one side in a show of exasperation. 'Not much,' I admitted. 'It was grey, I think, but beyond that, I was lying on the ground and trying to not wet myself.' Then I remembered the car it hit. 'I have a photo that might help back at the house.'

With my phone I had captured the red Audi A4 and the damage to it and, in several shots, also its number plate. 'Can you identify the make and model of the car that tried to hit me from the paint?'

DS Atwell frowned. 'Quite often, yes. Paint is relatively unique but even if I rush the process it might take a while.'

'What's a while? An hour? A month?'

'Days,' he replied. 'The severity of the crime and the priority attached to the evidence dictates the pecking order at the crime lab. There are two guys I get on with though, Steve and Simon, I'll have to see what I can bribe them with. We need to find the owner first though, easy now that we have the number plate, but I'll do it myself as the two boys outside will be busy with the ground team looking for evidence in the woods for the next few hours.'

'What do I do in the meantime?' I asked.

Mike grimaced. 'If I ask you to stay out of sight, will you do it?'

I choked on a laugh. 'I don't see how I can.'

'Then can you make sure you are never alone?'

I shook my head and made a sad face, the expression aimed at me rather than him. I had never felt so alone. The circle of friends I came to love and rely on were all on the Aurelia. There were hardly any people in the local area that I would call friends. Maggie was always the one but even if she wasn't dead, I couldn't look at her face again. Just as the self-pity began to take root, I saw it for what it was and stamped on it hard. 'I can't do that,' I told him. 'Instead, I think perhaps I'll just catch all the bad people, and have you lock them away. How does that sound?' Suddenly I was angry. Someone was trying to kill me which had to mean I was closing in on Maggie's killer. I didn't know who it was yet, but I had gotten too close for their liking and that had made me a target.

I was going to work it out and then I was going to close the net on them, whoever they were, even if my snooping led me right back to the Old City Firm.

Sensing my mood swing from helpless to remorseless, Detective Sergeant Mike Atwell backed away a pace. 'What just happened?' he asked.

I looked at him. 'Hmmm?'

'Your whole demeanour just went through a change. One second you looked forlorn and in need of a hug, the next you were giving out a vibe that made me want to be somewhere else. Do you do that often?'

I wasn't looking at him anymore, I was too busy thinking. 'I'm not sure,' I managed to mumble as I started toward the stairs. I needed to get a shower, get dressed and get going. I had people to see and questions to find answers to. 'Thank you for coming, Mike. Let yourself out, won't you?'

I didn't hear his answer if he gave one, nor did I hear him leave but both he and his car were gone by the time I came back down. Caution made me check outside for lurking murderers before I went out the front door, but no one tried to kill me before I got to my car. With Anna on the passenger seat, I set off for the lovely village of Marden, a twentyish minute drive through the villages. There I would find the parents of Mathew Hughes who I intended to grill for information about their son, his fiancée, the nature of his relationship with Maggie and a number of other things. I didn't think he was the killer any more than I thought Brevin and Drummond were, but they were all mixed up in this mystery somehow and none of them wanted me to find out how.

Embezzle and Run

Marden is a quaint little village on the way to Tonbridge from East Malling where I am. The houses were mostly expensive and desirable, although, like so many of the villages in Kent now, houses were going up in new estates bordering the village much to the disgruntlement of the original villagers. Most of the complaint was that the new houses were far cheaper and were thus bringing in a lower class of citizen, ones who might watch soccer instead of polo and who would ride motorbikes in favour of horses.

The Hughes' place was easy to find, sitting on the main road through the village as it did. It wasn't a large place; a country cottage built two hundred years ago or more, but it was quaint and would be filled with wonderful period features. The front garden was a postage stamp size but perfection nevertheless, with clipped rose trees rising up trellises either side of the door to form an arch above it and tidy flower beds bursting with autumn life.

The front door sat dead centre of the property with a window either side which would have made it an expensive property when it was built, not some worker's place. Before I could get to the door, it opened and a woman a little older than me appeared with a bucket in her left hand and a pair of secateurs in her right. 'Oh,' she said, caught by surprise on her way out.

I flashed her a warm smile. 'Hello. Are you Mrs Hughes? I'm Patricia Fisher.'

'Goodness, you are, aren't you?' she replied, looking me up and down. 'I read that you lived in this area.'

'Yes, I'm in East Malling. I hoped I might be able to talk to you about your son.'

She tilted her head as she looked at me, the request unexpected. 'Which one?' she asked.

Of course. It hadn't occurred to me to do the research Barbie or Jermaine would normally perform so I hadn't looked to see how many siblings Mathew might have. 'Mathew,' I replied. Then I frowned as I wondered how much Mrs Hughes knew. 'You do know that his boss was murdered recently, right?'

'Yes, yes. That awful Margaret Jeffries. I met her once at a dinner party, all she did was ogle my husband.' That sounded like Maggie alright. 'I'm Rose, how can I help you?'

Rose led me back inside her house, which had a low ceiling, built, as it was, so long ago that the human race was six inches shorter. Neither of us were tall enough that we needed to duck to get under the oak joists in the ceiling, but I only had a couple of inches to spare. The kitchen was in the back where she had a dining table set up to look out over an equally pretty back garden. She abandoned her plan to prune the roses to instead fill the kettle and take a short break.

Coming through the house, she told me her husband was out at the local supermarket getting supplies and I explained my desire to contact Mathew.

'He's in Bali with Sophia,' she told me.

I wanted to ask if she was sure about that, but held back, choosing to apply a little more tact instead when I asked, 'Have you heard from him?'

'Only once. He called about a week ago to let me know they were having a great time and the weather was splendid.'

I got Mathew's number from Graham at the office yesterday but didn't get a chance to call it until less than an hour ago. Basically, it slipped my mind yesterday with everything that had happened, but there was a big fat clue when I did this morning: I didn't get an international dial tone. I got a UK dial tone instead. He wasn't in Bali at all.

He didn't answer the call and none of these things made him guilty of anything, but if you are lying about one thing... 'Can you call him now, Rose?'

She looked up from putting teabags into a teapot, her face showing surprise at my request. She didn't argue though. 'Um, yes, sure. What is it you want me to ask him?'

Her phone was in her right trouser pocket, stuffed in with a small lady's handkerchief which tumbled to the floor when she took the phone out. She hadn't noticed and I paid it no mind as I watched her swipe the screen and press a few buttons. She put the phone to her ear. 'Can you put it on speakerphone, please?' I asked.

This time she frowned at my request, feeling, I thought, that I was beginning to intrude. She did it though and we both heard the familiar UK dial tone. She hadn't noticed the incongruity though until I pointed it out to her. Now she was really frowning. 'I guess he came back early.'

The phone continued to ring.

'Did you get an international dial tone last time?' I asked.

She shook her head. 'He phoned me. I don't call him very often because he always moans that he is working.'

The phone continued to ring. Then, just as I felt it had to switch to voicemail, it was answered, a breezy young woman's voice, 'Hello, Rose, are you after Mattie?'

'Oh, hello, Sophia…' Rose had placed the phone on the dining table so I could hear it as requested, but now I held a hand up to beg for quiet so I could talk.

'Sophia, are you in Bali?'

She didn't answer right away, the new voice she didn't recognise confused her. 'Who is this?' she asked, no trace of concern in her voice, just curiosity because someone unknown was asking her questions.

'Are you in Bali, Sophia?' I repeated, aware that I was being rude but too close to the truth to worry about it. Then we heard a commotion, a man's voice, raised and upset, demanding to know why she was answering his phone? It clicked and went dead.

Rose looked up at me, her eyes wide. 'What's going on?'

I fixed her with an even stare, trying to work out if she was doing a good job of bluffing me or genuinely had no idea what her son was involved in. I could detect no subterfuge behind her eyes. 'Mathew is mixed up in what happened to Maggie.' It was a bold statement which made her gasp and I knew she was about to start denying that he could be, so I got in first. 'I don't know to what extent and I am not suggesting that he is guilty of her murder or even of playing a part in it. I think though, that something he has done may have resulted in events that culminated in her murder.' In truth I thought her death might be completely unrelated, but I wanted to speak to him to help me work out what had been happening and his mother was my route to achieve that. 'You need to help me find him; he may be in great danger.'

My words suitably terrified her, jolting her from the table where she was leaning. Then the kettle clicked off, the noise loud in the quiet kitchen and that made her jump. With a hand pressed to her chest to still her thumping heart, she asked, 'What do you need me to do?'

I asked her to call him back but, as expected, his phone was now off, and the calls went straight to voicemail. The direct approach wasn't going to work so some good, old-fashioned, detective work was needed. 'Tell me about his fiancée, please?'

Rose Hughes was only too happy to tell me all about the lovely Sophia, a girl she clearly thought of as a daughter already. Pictures on her walls showed a family filled with sons, the three boys close in age, but each separated by a year or more if their comparative heights were a good indicator. Rose talked about Mathew's fiancée as if she was the daughter she never had, grabbing a framed photo of the couple from the mantlepiece to show me. Sophia came from money, something Rose didn't say but intimated when she talked about her parents and their property in the countryside near Guildford in Surrey. I got the same story from Graham yesterday, so Mathew had bagged himself a pretty girl who stood to inherit a fortune as the only child of a self-made millionaire. None of that had anything to do with Maggie so far as I could see.

We talked around the subject for most of an hour before she asked a question I wished she had started with, 'Will it help if we check his bank account?'

Instantly attentive, I asked, 'You can do that?'

Rose and I were both sitting at the dining table still, our cups of tea empty and pushed to one side, but she rose and took two paces to snag a laptop from the kitchen counter. 'He was always rubbish with money as a teenager, so I had parental access to his accounts. I don't touch them now, but I doubt he has bothered to change the passwords.' I was holding my breath as she entered a sequence of digits. My initial thoughts on this case had all been to do with money. Charlie taking out a large sum right before she died only strengthened that belief and DS Atwell told me the accounts were patchy, sums disappearing over the course of nine months he said only to be suddenly replaced and then taken out again.

'How long has Mathew been courting Sophia?' I asked.

Rose thought about it for a second, using her fingers to work backward. 'We met her at Christmas but I think they had been dating for a couple of months then, meeting the mother is what you do after the fact these days.' She hadn't answered the question and took a second to realise that herself. 'Sorry, about nine or ten months, I think.'

It tallied. According to Charlie, there were only three people with access to the accounts anyway. Charlie, Maggie, and Mathew. The first two were unlikely culprits which left Mathew and until I knew what he was using it for, I couldn't determine if it was linked to the case or not.

Rose turned the laptop so I could see it. It displayed a box on the right which listed different accounts. There were three of them, one of which had twelve pence in it, one which looked like savings with just over three hundred pounds in and a current account which held almost twenty thousand pounds. It was an unusually large sum to have in a current account. Who needed that much readily available money? It was a rhetorical question which was only asked inside my head because I already knew the answer: a person on the run.

What was yet more interesting were the recent transactions. They showed me where he was, right down to the address. Okay, it didn't actually show me the address, but the deposit taken on a debit card swipe at the Seascape Hotel in Margate was a clear enough signpost for me. It was taken almost two weeks ago so he had been hiding out there ever since. More recent transactions for meals and incidentals showed that he was still in the area. Guess where I was going next?

'Can we look back at his expenditure over the last few months?'

'I'm as curious as you are,' murmured Rose as she clicked a box and began scrolling. Her son was up to something and she didn't know what it was; a mother's suspicious instinct was kicking into high gear now as we both saw the money coming into and going out of his account.

Six weeks ago, there was a sudden injection of ten thousand pounds. A month before that a further eight thousand. It went on like that. Money arriving in large, exact sums and then going out again over the following few weeks as he frittered it away. There was a regular payment to an Aston Martin dealership. When Rose saw that, she said, 'He told me the car was a bonus from Maggie.'

He had lied because it was costing him almost two thousand a month. On top of that there were regular payments to a florist, each time for over a hundred pounds which had to be quite the bouquet, and lots of high price meals out in named London restaurants. I knew what he was doing: he was romancing the rich girl, playing up to her aspirations, or, more likely, what he imagined her aspirations to be. She probably just wanted a man to love her, but perhaps she was superficial and materialistic. I might never know, but what was clear was how much money he was spending.

'Any idea how much he earns?' I asked.

She shook her head. 'No. It's quite a bit though.' Quite a bit depended entirely on one's perspective of course. There were people I met on board the Aurelia who wouldn't get out of bed for less than a million. Whatever he earned, I was convinced the large sums coming in would prove to be money embezzled from Maggie's firm. I was also willing to bet

Superintendent Jenkins hadn't even bothered to look at Mathew as a credible suspect so had failed to uncover the embezzlement or that he had skipped town. Each sum came from the same account number. If I showed them to Charlie, he would be able to confirm whether it was Jeffries Imperial Publishing or not, though I was going to be surprised if it wasn't.

Whatever the case, my next task was to track him down and now I knew where he was.

'Rose, thank you for your time and for your help,' I said as I gathered my notepad, pen, and phone.

She rose to see me out. 'Not at all. If there's anything more I can do to help, please call me. I don't know what he has got himself into, but I want him home safely. Can you do that?'

It was an unfair question. I'm just one woman and I'm trying to solve a murder. How exactly am I supposed to protect a grown man? Especially since his greatest enemies appear to be his own greed and stupidity. I promised to do my best though, slid into my battered old Ford Fiesta and turned the key.

It's strange that only at that point, when the motor was running, did I think about the killer stalking me. Two attempts on my life in less than twenty-four hours, but only now did I wonder whether someone might put a bomb in my car.

It didn't explode though, the engine ticking over a little erratically but alive just the same. Little did I know that there are other, less suspicious, ways to tinker with a car yet make it just as deadly.

Margate

On the drive to Margate, a delightful seaside town a good hour south from Marden, I had time and quiet to have another go at piecing things together. Maggie had been murdered in an execution style hit thirteen days ago. She had also been visited by a pair of well-known and reputedly ruthless East End Gangsters just hours before her death. There were holes in her accounts where money had been going out though I felt certain Mathew Hughes, her office manager, was to blame for that. Then a sudden influx of money I could not account for and barely a day later a hundred grand going back out again, this time because Charlie took it to pay bills. To assume Brevin and Drummond were to blame or somehow involved seemed obvious, yet I believed their plea of innocence. I had to wonder though, if perhaps they had put up the money that suddenly reappeared in her business account. It was a large sum, not the sort of cash many people have lying around unless you are in organised crime and have money lending as one of your lucrative enterprises. My tentative conclusion was that Mathew had taken the money, known he needed to cover the gap before someone noticed and borrowed it from the Old City Firm.

Why though? Why would Mathew Hughes go to a money lender for money that was going to cost an actual arm and a leg if he didn't pay it back on time? That was the part that I couldn't work out. It just didn't fit. He was clearly a bright man and entrusted with running a successful business so was obviously business astute. Loan sharks were the fodder of the desperate, of people with nowhere else to turn.

If I could find him, then I could ask him. Phoning the hotel in advance to get his room number occurred to me, as did trying to get through to him on the room's landline: if I could get my answers over the phone, I could avoid a lengthy journey in a less than trustworthy car. I thought it more likely I would spook him though, so the longer route to success was the one I took.

I also made a call to Charlie. There was one question he might be able to answer, but my car wasn't a model fitted with handsfree phone stuff, so I had to pull into a layby to make the call. He answered sounding annoyed that I had called, 'Hello, Patricia, what can I do for you?' He said all the right words but without the correct tone attached to them.

'How much does Mathew Hughes earn?' I asked, getting directly to the point.

'About a hundred and twenty grand a year the last time I looked. It might be slightly more than that now.'

I let out a low whistle of appreciation. It was a decent amount for a man in his early thirties to be taking home, but then he worked in the city where everything cost twice as much and it probably wasn't that great of a wage compared to many people running businesses. 'Okay, Charlie. Thank you.' I disconnected, put the car back in gear and set off again.

The Margate Seascape Hotel's name wasn't a clever marketing ploy where guests discovered their rooms actually looked out onto the back of another building. It occupied a commanding position overlooking the sea with uninterrupted views. It looked both old, in that I was certain it had been erected early in the twentieth century, art deco touches giving its age away, but also brand new, in that it appeared to have undergone a massive facelift in recent times. Above all, it screamed swanky.

I swung up to the front door to use the valet parking, the valet doing his best not to turn his face up at my tired old car. Keys were exchanged for a ticket and the doorman held the door for me.

Inside, the hotel was just as lovely, polished marble floor stretching from the door across a large lobby to a reception desk manned by four people. I bypassed them to go directly to the concierge desk where a man in his forties, wearing a very nice suit, did his utmost to look happy to see me.

I wasted no time at all. 'Hello, I'm Patricia Fisher,' I started.

'Goodness, yes, so you are. The Margate Seascape Hotel is honoured to have you here. Will you be staying with us long?'

'Sorry, no. I'm here investigating a murder and need to speak with one of your guests.' His eyes flared in mute surprise, but I pressed on. 'I'm here ahead of the police, but they will be along soon if I am not able to convince your guests to leave.' I played it for the win; I needed to talk to Mathew Hughes, and the concierge would do anything to keep the police from breaking down doors and disturbing all the guests. There is such a thing as bad publicity despite what marketers might say.

His eyes looked down a computer on his desk. 'The name of the guest, madam?'

'Mathew Hughes.'

'Ah, yes. He's in our honeymoon suite. Shall I escort you?'

I shook my head. 'Please, just point the way.'

He came out from behind his desk anyway, escorting me to the elevator where he pressed the call button. 'The honeymoon suite is the only room on the top floor and the elevator opens directly into it. The button for it can only be accessed with an additional card given to the residents. Or,' he produced a key, 'an override key.'

Inside the elevator car he operated the control, used his key and went back to his desk without looking back as the door closed. For once I didn't feel nervous. This part of the investigation ought to be a civilised conversation.

The elevator pinged its arrival on the top floor and the doors began to open. Then a vase flew over my head to smash against the wall behind me, showering me in water, shards of pottery and bits of flower. Inside the lobby of the honeymoon suite a full-blown battle was taking place.

Lovers' Tiff

Just ahead, a man with his back to me, cowered in nothing but a pair of socks. He had a shirt and trousers balled in his right hand and was poised to evade the next missile. Across the room from him stood a small blonde woman I recognised from Rose's framed photograph as Sophia. Her chest heaved beneath her tear streaked face. She, at least, was covered, though all she had on was a negligee. The bottom pointing my way had to belong to Mathew Hughes though I couldn't tell it was him from the current view.

I had managed to interrupt the mother of all lovers' tiffs.

Sophia saw me, pointed an accusing finger in my direction, and shouted, 'Is she another one of them?' Then she screamed in rage and stormed from the room.

Mathew spun around to see who was there, his todger swinging from left to right, propelled by the inertia though I did my very best to keep my eyes focused firmly on his face. 'Who are you?' he demanded angrily. Actually, he didn't say, "Who are you?" he added in a few extra words I have edited out for brevity but I'm sure you can imagine what they were.

Still looking at his face, though the damned appendage wouldn't stop wiggling about, I said in a calm voice. 'I'm here to save your life, Mathew. You should get changed so we can talk.' He eyed me sternly, looking every part fuelled by anger and ready to throw me out. 'Or, I can call Brevin and Drummond if you prefer.'

It was a wild guess on my part, throwing the names out to see how he reacted. Either I would get no reaction because he had no idea who Brevin and Drummond were, or I would get what I hoped for. As the colour drained from his face and his thingy shrunk and looked for a place to hide, I performed a mental fist pump: I had guessed right again, and I was on my way to solving this case.

I held up a hand with a single finger pointing down and twirled it in a circle to indicate that he should turn around. I wanted him to put some clothes on. Silently, but with a big gulp before he moved, Mathew Hughes left the lobby with me following not too closely behind his bare behind.

Somewhere deeper in the suite, Sophia was still spitting fire and screaming rage. As he neared the bedroom, she burst out of it, dressed but looking a little dishevelled, her outfit selection, hair and makeup no doubt performed in record time. Dragging behind in her right hand was a pink suitcase that was almost as big as her and probably weighed more. She paused, ripped off her engagement ring and threw it at him. 'You can keep that, Mathew,' she spat. Of course, she used a different word in place of his name, but, well, I'm sure you understand the flavour of the conversation.

She was storming out, so I moved to stop her, thankful that I at least had size and weight on my side. 'Hold on, Sophia, I need to talk to you.'

Her face filled with rage and she dropped the suitcase, letting it hang in the air for second as it tried to decide whether to stand up or fall, choosing after a half second of indecision to crash to the carpet behind her. By then she was advancing on me, both hands up: she was going to attack me! The realisation dawned just as it crossed my mind that her diminutive size didn't mean she wasn't dangerous. She could be a black belt for all I knew.

'Whoa!' I protested, taking a step back. 'I haven't done anything to you, Sophia. I'm here to help.' My protests fell on deaf ears; she was beyond reason but mercifully, when she leapt at me, it was like being attacked by an angry toddler. I grabbed both her wrists as she tried to hit me, easily holding them in place while I begged for calm.

Seeing the madness ensuing six feet away, Mathew, still naked, stepped in to pull his fiancée away. However, cooing at her to be calm only riled her even further, the tiny woman thrashing about to free herself from my grip, which she succeeded in doing only to swing an unaimed kick backward to connect with Mathews soft parts.

He made an, 'Ooof,' noise as he folded in on himself and sagged to the floor. Sophia paused, making me think for a moment that she was going to comfort him. She didn't though, she seized her opportunity to do real damage, grabbed a heavy brass ornament from the coffee table and lifted it high above her head with murder on her mind.

I snatched it from her grip in mid-air. 'Really, Sophia, you need to calm down so we can talk.'

Finally, the dam burst, and she sank onto the couch behind her in a sobbing fit of tears.

I breathed a sigh of relief because for the first time since the elevator doors opened, no one was about to get killed by something. 'Mathew,' I begged, 'can you please go and put some clothes on?'

Shamefaced and hobbling the whole way, Mathew struggled to the bedroom door and vanished inside. On the couch, Sophia had dissolved into a soggy mess. 'Why does this always happen to me?' she wailed, demanding an answer from the sky or God or anyone who felt like answering. 'Why can't men just be faithful? It's really not that hard.'

I wanted to say something cool like, 'I hear you, sister,' but it sounded daft even in my head and would probably get a curious expression rather than a fist bump. Instead, I settled for, 'How did you find out?'

'About his cheating?' Sophia looked up at me with tear-swollen eyes. 'Was that you on the phone earlier? Asking me if we were in Bali?'

'Yes, it was.'

She nodded, taking a moment to dig in her handbag for a pack of tissues. She blew her nose loudly and wiped her face. 'God, I must look a sight. How is it that I keep letting boys do this to me? I think I have found the one, but they always turn out to be just like the rest.' She let out a big shuddering sigh and sagged back even further into the couch so it was all but swallowing her. 'I knew there was something odd going on even before you called. Why on earth were we staying in a hotel in Margate for goodness sake? I mean, it's nice enough, but Bali would be more like it.'

I didn't have an answer to that question, but I prompted her again about the infidelity. 'What do you know about his cheating, Sophia?'

Another shuddering sigh escaped her body. 'I confronted him after he snatched the phone from me and hung up. It was obvious he had told people we were going to Bali, so I wanted to know why I was stuck in Margate. I asked if it was something to do with his boss getting murdered. That happened like two days after we got here. He got a message from someone at the office, but he didn't react at all other than to be very quiet for several days and then massively overcompensate by taking me out shopping. He should have been running back to the office to steady the ship, but he didn't even call them back. And he was most insistent that we couldn't use social media while we were away. He made a game of it, wanting me to pretend it was the 1920s and mobile phones didn't exist. We were having a pretend honeymoon he said; two weeks in Margate like a well-to-do couple might have back then. No phones, no social media, just us and...'

'Yes?' I prompted.

'And the bedroom,' she finished her sentence with a shame-filled face. 'Two weeks is up tomorrow, and I kept asking him what he was going to do next and never once got an answer. It was when I pushed him about his boss though, that was when I could tell. Call it a woman's intuition if you like, or maybe it's just that every other man has done it to me, but I knew. He was being so evasive. When I asked him outright if he had been sleeping with her, he denied it and I knew he was lying.' She looked me in the eyes for the first time. 'I'm sorry you had to walk in on that.'

I accepted her apology though it was not necessary for her to give one. 'What else did he tell you?'

She blew out a sigh before starting to talk. 'That he doesn't earn as much as he told me; not even nearly. He had this ridiculous idea that I needed to be pampered and constantly presented with gifts. All I wanted was for him to keep it in his pants.' She looked up at my face again. 'Is he in trouble?' she asked.

I took my time to answer. 'I don't know. He might be. I need to ask him some questions.'

'Do you need me?' she clearly wanted to leave.

I thought about that. 'Do you know the names Jim Brevin or Ian Drummond?'

She shook her head slowly from side to side. 'Should I?'

'Probably not.'

'Can I go?'

'I can't stop you, Sophia. I'm not the police and you haven't committed a crime that I know of. Mrs Hughes will be upset; she has quite the soft spot for you.'

She smiled at me. 'Yeah, I really like her. Maybe I should sleep with one of his brothers so I get to continue seeing her. That would really stick it to Mathew, wouldn't it?'

I didn't know if she was serious or not, but I had to agree that it really would be an apt punishment. Just as Sophia rose to leave the room, Mathew sheepishly stuck his head out of the bedroom. 'Don't go, Sophia,' he begged.

As she twirled on the spot to deliver her retort, I quickly escaped to the lobby, my fingers in my ears so I wouldn't hear what she had to say to him. A few moments later she strode past me with her head held high. 'He's all yours,' she said as she jabbed the button for the elevator and left his life for good.

I found him sitting at a two-chair table by the window in the penthouse honeymoon suite. He was staring out the window at nothing in particular, his expression somewhere between utterly forlorn and hopelessly lost. He didn't bother to look at me when he spoke. 'I expected them to send someone bigger. Or are they waiting outside for Sophia to leave before they come in to cut off my fingers and toes?'

I sat in the other chair. 'There's no one here but me, Mathew.' His head snapped around, shocked at the news and instantly hopeful that he might yet get away. It was cruel of me to do so, but also efficient so I chose to use his fear of the Old City Firm to get the information I needed. 'That can change very quickly, Mathew. You are lucky that at this point no one has paid a visit to your mother. These are very serious people you are dealing with.'

He sighed forlornly. 'I know. I underestimated them.'

'You were sleeping with Maggie, weren't you?' It came out as a question because I wanted him to confirm it. It didn't really matter whether he was or not, I didn't think it would have much sway on events past; it was time to fill in the blanks though.

He nodded rather than speak, but after a few seconds, he added, 'Yes.'

'Why did you borrow money from gangsters?' This was a critical question so far as I was concerned.

He picked at his nails, looking sick. 'I thought I could convince them to let me keep it. There's no way a bank would, and I had... felt I had good reason to believe they would waive the paltry sum I borrowed.'

'Paltry sum? Wasn't it a hundred grand that you borrowed? Hadn't you embezzled almost that much and now needed to get it back before anyone noticed?'

He showed no sign of having even heard me, but again, after a few seconds, he nodded his head.

'So you took the money from the business account knowing no one else would notice and borrowed it from two men who would dice you into pieces if you crossed them. What made you think that they would let you off with the money?' I couldn't be more curious to hear this part of the puzzle.

He put his head in his hands. 'I had something I knew they would want. Something they would want to be sure no one else ever saw. Once I had the money, I showed it to them and offered to let them have it if they forgot about my loan. I even threatened to publish what I had on the internet if they didn't agree.'

My jaw dropped. 'You tried to blackmail two of the most hardened criminals in London?'

'Yeah,' he admitted, the tone of his voice letting me know that he recognised how foolish that had been.

I placed a hand on his arm. 'Mathew, you have to tell me what it is and what this has to do with Maggie. I don't know if I can save you, but we need to solve her murder and get you into protective custody where the police can put you in a witness protection program or something. Did you have evidence of a crime?' In my head, if he threatened to use it as leverage to be let off the loan, he had to have come across something that would put Brevin and Drummond away forever. Now at least I knew why he borrowed money from such an awful pair; he thought he could get away without paying it back. When I got no answer, I shook his arm. 'Hey, Mathew, you need to tell me how this led to Maggie's death.'

'I don't know,' he wailed, a tear rolling down each cheek. 'I don't know why they killed her unless it was just revenge. I don't think they knew about the photos until I sent them the email.'

I pricked up my ears. 'Photos? What photos?' Was this the evidence he had? A series of pictures showing them killing someone maybe?

'You have to understand; Maggie was just a bit of fun. For both of us, I mean. Neither wanted anything from the other. It started right after the interview, years ago. She interviewed me at her office in London, not the one the firm works out of now, but the old one. She told me I might get called forward for a final interview and when she did call, she wanted me to come to her house in Kent. Of course I went, but the second interview was more of a... physical examination.' I didn't need him to draw me a picture, I knew what she was like with men. 'It was a great job, I was so excited, but I knew it wasn't great pay for the sector. She kept me dangling with promises of shares, a partnership if you will and I knew that was worth far more than any pay rise I could ever get. That went on for years and I just couldn't take it anymore. I needed more money just to keep up with my outgoings and I met Sophia and I knew I couldn't keep her happy on my pathetic wage. Not in London. So, I took the extra money I needed. A little at first, just a few thousand out of the account. We spent so much on marketing I was sure no one would ever notice. And they didn't, so I took some more and then some more. I even told myself I deserved it, but I suddenly realised I had eaten through nearly a hundred thousand pounds and when she found out, I wouldn't get a partnership, I would get sacked for embezzling. I had to get the money back and I had to keep up the pretence with her. I went to her house once a week. The team believed it was a weekly strategy meeting between me and the two directors. It wasn't though. It was just sex. Afterwards she would ask me about the business and I would tell her the truth about how we were doing and the truth about how much money the firm was making but lie about the buoyancy of the accounts because it was missing almost a hundred grand.'

'Then what happened?'

'Then she gave me the golden ticket. She had been out for a boozy lunch drinking gin with one of her friends and was on the champagne by the time I arrived. Lying in bed afterwards, she bragged about old connections with East End gangsters, proper hard men that killed their business rivals because that was efficient. It wasn't the first time she talked about business like that, but this time I could hear that it wasn't hyperbole; she actually knew the men she was talking about. I asked her how and she launched into a long story about getting mugged one night when she lived up there. She was walking home and a little tipsy but two men came to her rescue.'

I remembered now that Maggie might have lived in Kent most of her life, but she had also worked in London for most of it. She moved up there for a couple of years in her early twenties and would have been out at night in bars and clubs the same as any other woman her age. There was an obvious conclusion coming, so I made it for him, 'Those two men, her rescuers, they were Jim Brevin and Ian Drummond, weren't they?'

Mathew nodded. 'She decided to repay them in a traditional manner.' I bet she did. That sounded just like Maggie. 'but she took pictures. She had one of those old instant cameras that spits the picture out the bottom once it's taken.'

'A polaroid camera?'

'Is that what it's called? She had one anyway and they got drunk and did drugs and she had photographs of these two men having sex with her and having sex with each other and she was drunk enough that afternoon with me to tell me where she kept them.'

'And you used them for blackmail.'

He nodded again, his head still in his hands. 'I thought they would be pleased to have them back safe in their hands. I was going to keep a few of the good shots for insurance. You know, to make sure they knew they couldn't make me disappear once I handed them over.'

'Which would put them forever in your pocket.'

'Yeah, I hadn't thought about that. They gave me two weeks to come up with the money; that was the original loan period and if I did that, and handed over the pictures, they would only kill me. Otherwise they would kill everyone I know: my mum and dad, Sophia, her mum and dad, all the people at work. They knew names and addresses by the time they answered me.'

This was such a mess. 'Where are the pictures now, Mathew?'

A mournful sigh escaped his lips. 'In my car.'

I felt like berating him for his stupidity. I itched to take a book and whack him on the head many times. The people he had crossed were not the sort to forgive.

'Do you have the money?' I asked.

He sobbed into his hands. 'No. I went to get it back out of the firm's account, but it had already gone, every last penny I had paid back in plus a little bit more.' Yes, Charlie had taken it.

'Surely there's more money in the firm's account.'

'Not that kind of capital. Our cash account never has anything like that much in it. Plus, to get that kind of cash requires at least one of the directors to sign the paperwork.'

'When is the deadline up?'

'Tomorrow.' He put his arms on the tabletop and buried his head in them. 'They're going to cut me into little pieces and make me eat them until there's nothing left of me but the bit left to eat with.' He was bordering on hysterical now.

'I need the pictures, Mathew. Give me your car keys.' He wasn't able to speak but he yanked keys from his trouser pocket. 'Where in the car are they?' He just shook his head, unable to make words or make sense, or do anything. I figured I could find them, so I left the room and went to the elevator. Then I stopped and went back, locked the door that led to the balcony sitting a dozen floors above the pavement of Margate and took the key with me. It wouldn't stop him from killing himself another way, of course, so I placed a hand on his shoulder and said, 'We can get you out of this yet, Mathew. Just hold on for a few more hours.'

The photographs were in an envelope in the glove box of his beautiful Aston Martin. I expected it to be a new car, but it was vintage instead. I didn't know what it was, but it looked to be fifty years old or more and it was the most elegant piece of automotive engineering I had ever seen. The pictures were also vintage and also in great condition. It was the late eighties; I could tell by Maggie's hairstyle which I remembered her styling after a band who were in the charts at the time. It took an hour to create each time, intense backcombing required just to get the volume. I didn't look through many of the photographs, just enough to be certain I had the right thing. I could see why two hard men from London would kill for them. If these got out, it would ruin their reputations, most likely end their marriages, if they were indeed married, and possibly cause their criminal empire to crumble.

They got tucked back into the envelope and buried at the bottom of my handbag. It hadn't occurred to me to ask for the access key, so I needed the concierge to get me up to the top floor again. His furtive eyes were checking all around to see if anyone was listening as he walked with me to the elevator once more. 'Do I, ah, do I need to prepare the manager?'

'For a police raid? No, I don't think so. I believe Mr Hughes will be checking out early though.'

'Yes, I saw his girlfriend leave earlier. She seemed to be in a hurry.'

I thanked him as he operated the button for the top floor again and promised that I would also be leaving soon. With the door closed, I said a silent prayer that I would find Mathew still alive and breathing, a sigh of relief escaping my lips when he proved to be both.

Dealing with him was nothing to do with my investigation. I was being paid to solve Maggie's murder and this wasn't part of it. However, I now felt certain I knew why Brevin and Drummond visited her house; it happened right after Mathew foolishly used the pictures in a bid to blackmail them, perhaps they never knew they existed, perhaps they did and trusted Maggie with them but the former felt more likely. They went to her house to ask about them and hours later she was dead. It wasn't conclusive but suddenly they had revenge as a motive for murder. I could understand them taking it personally and their anger boiling over into hiring a contract killer. Heck, they probably had a couple on their books they could just send. Either way she was dead now, and they were back as my prime suspects. Their request that I not look into them was an attempt to convince me to leave the case alone. They felt they could handle the police, but I was the wildcard. That was what Superintendent Jenkins called me too.

So now I had a moral dilemma. To take them down I was going to have to keep Mathew and all his friends and family safe as well as make sure I had enough evidence to secure an arrest and conviction. That seemed like a tough choice. Or I could bargain with them, get the money from Charlie and give them that and the pictures with a request that they now leave everyone alone.

Would they go for that?

I had serious doubts.

In fact, I thought it highly likely the car that tried to squish me last night and the archer shooting arrows at my head this morning were both at the hands of the man with no neck and sent by the Old City Firm. It was a horrifying thought.

Mathew hadn't moved in the time it took me to get to his car and back. 'We need to get going,' I insisted. 'You can't stay here. You are in enough debt already.'

'Where are we going?' he asked. 'I can't escape through any of the airports, they said they have men everywhere looking for me. I didn't really believe them, but I didn't want to chance it either, that's why I am hiding in Margate.'

'It took me an hour to find you when I started looking, Mathew. The only reason they haven't tracked you here is because your time isn't up yet. All that will change tomorrow so we need to get you back to the local police and into some kind of custody where you can be protected.'

'They own the police,' he argued.

I remembered what Jim and Ian boasted: they had men inside Superintendent Jenkins' team. 'Perhaps in London, but not in the countryside.' Thinking of DS Atwell, I said, 'I have someone I trust.'

I had to kick his chair to get him moving but he stuffed his belongings into a suitcase and a holdall and trudged out of the honeymoon suite behind me. He was going to follow my car back from the hotel to Maidstone police station where a single phone call had arranged for DS Atwell to meet us.

The valet returned my rickety old car while Mathew paid his final bill at reception. Then I waited for his distinctive car to appear and set off with his forlorn face in my rear-view mirror.

A mile outside Margate, once we were doing seventy on the M2 motorway, the thing with my car happened. Not the thing where it coughs, clatters and breaks down. Oh no, nothing so benign. No, it did the thing where a wall of flame suddenly erupts from beneath the bonnet to engulf the entire front end of the car.

I damned near wet my knickers.

How Many Attempts is That?

Screaming didn't seem to achieve much so when I ran out of oxygen, I did what I could to check traffic despite the flames licking around my door mirrors, gave up, and swung the steering wheel. I went from the fast lane to the hard shoulder in one move, a few horns tracking my passage, but I survived the move and heard no terrible rending of metal sounds to indicate I had just caused a ten-car pile-up.

I slammed on my brake pedal, but nothing happened, and it was at this point when the panic really settled in. I couldn't see and I couldn't stop. What exactly was I supposed to do? Open the door, hope the flames didn't get me and jump for it?

Some subliminal, primitive part of my brain kicked in, screaming at me to change down the gears. It would retard the engine or something like that. I shifted from fourth to third and then down to second almost straight away. The engine screamed in protest, I was doing it no good at all, but who was I kidding? This car was toast. If I got out alive, I would need a new car because whether I lived or not, I doubted the car could.

The car was slowing though, gear ratios or something doing their job but just as I allowed a faint glimmer of hope to enter my thoughts, the heat from the flames caused the windscreen to crack. If it exploded, it wouldn't just be glass I had to contend with! I yanked on the handbrake, mercifully discovering that it still worked, and the car began to grind inexorably to a halt with the back wheels locked up.

Even before it got to walking pace, my handbag was tucked under my arm and I had my hand on the door release handle. Just before it stopped, I risked it, throwing the door open, saying a prayer and letting myself flop out onto the road with a quick glance back up the inside lane to see if there was a juggernaut coming.

I read somewhere once that in an accident the worst thing to do was tense up and because of that I made myself as floppy as I could. Ten seconds later when I finally stopped bouncing and spinning, I promised myself I would find that quote, find the person that wrote it, and make them eat my handbag.

I was alive though.

Somehow, I was still alive. This was the third attempt on my life in twenty-four hours, each one using a different method and each one coming close to doing the job. Behind my car, a large truck pulled to a stop with a screech of tyres, the driver bailing out to come to my rescue. He wasn't the only one. Mathew, who I figured would just keep driving until he reached Greenland, the North Pole or somewhere equally remote, had parked on the hard shoulder a hundred yards beyond my car and was running back toward me.

Ten minutes later the cops arrived along with an ambulance and the fire brigade. The whole motorway was closed in both directions, the incident making the evening national news because of the tail backs it caused and the dashcam footage of a middle-aged woman diving out of a still moving, burning car. When the freelance reporter that followed the emergency services to the scene found out the woman was Patricia Fisher, he was instantly on the phone to every paper, radio, and newspaper station he could think of. I denied him the interview he wanted, knowing it would bring me no benefit and because I knew I must look terrible.

Once the fire was out, a firefighter cautiously opened the bonnet and found the cause of the fire: there was a small cut in the fuel pipe running to my car's fuel injection system. I was certain it had been done deliberately, but it was such an old car that the pipe could simply have perished and there was so much damage from the fire no one would ever prove otherwise. I had to listen to advice about making sure my car was regularly serviced by a qualified mechanic. However, the hole in the pipe was in the perfect place to ensure it would leak petrol onto the exhaust manifold, so once the manifold reached critical temperature, which was right when I got on the motorway, it ignited the constant jet of fuel and caused the fire. There was no way to prove it had been done deliberately but I knew it had; the man with no neck had struck again. How many failed attempts would there be before he got lucky?

I was in so much trouble. Where was Jermaine when I needed him? The answer to that particular question was, of course, on board the Aurelia and bound for Cork in Ireland.

Mathew waited for the police to finish questioning me. There was no reason to detain me, so I was free to go and despite having no car, I still had a lift to get to where I wanted to go. It was late afternoon now and I had more than two dozen pieces of sticking plaster on me where the paramedics had done what they could. They wanted to take me to hospital for a full check-up, but I refused, largely based on the certain knowledge that they don't serve gin in hospital. I was bruised and battered, I had dozens of scrapes and abrasions, but it was all insignificant.

Once I was in the car, he asked the question he hadn't wanted to pose in front of the police. 'Was that them?'

I closed my eyes and nodded. 'I think so.' Whoever it was, they were able to track me and kept coming up with different ways to kill me. I no longer believed it was a vengeful wife or a desperate husband who had killed Maggie and was now coming after me to stop me finding the truth. Nor did I believe it was a contract killer sent by one of the people whose guilt I had revealed during my time away. The Old City Firm were too present and dangerous. They were right in the middle of this and they wanted me to die far away from them where no connection could be made.

'They're going to kill us, aren't they?' he stammered, utterly terrified.

My eyes snapped open. 'No!' I was squinting into nothingness as my brain began to see a vague hint of a plan. 'No, they won't get the chance.'

'How are you going to stop them?' he wailed.

I turned my head to face him. 'By being cleverer than them. Start the car, Mathew. It's time to ruin their day.'

With reluctant hands, Mathew turned the key of his car. It roared to life in a surprising way, the seat vibrating under my bottom in a not unpleasant manner. My attention distracted, I asked, 'What is this car?'

'An Aston Martin DB2/4 Drophead Coupé,' he replied, equally distracted by it clearly as a smile played across his lips. 'It's really rare.' As he pulled out onto the motorway and started building up speed, I looked around the car's sleek interior. Everything about it was refined and conservative from the beautiful wooden dashboard to the supple tan leather seats. There were two seats behind me as well, though one would never fit an adult into them. Mathew saw me looking about and continued talking, 'It was a production car in the 50s made here in England though the convertible model we are in was an option some owners took after they bought it. The conversion was performed under license by Bertone. It is slow by modern standards and heavy on fuel consumption, but I think that is a small price to pay for such a beautiful car.'

'It is very elegant,' I agreed.

'Do you know this is the same car Tippi Hendren drove in Alfred Hitchcock's movie, *The Birds*?'

I remembered the movie but not the car. It wasn't the time for discussing movies and motors though, we still had to get out of the current pickle we were in and that meant I had phone calls to make.

Setting Things Up

Detective Sergeant Mike Atwell answered on the first ring. 'Patricia? I have the television on, and it says your car just burst into flames on the M2 motorway.'

I sighed. 'Yes. That's me.' On top of everything else, I now needed to go car shopping. 'I think it safe to assume the attempt to barbecue me in my car was perpetrated by the same person to shoot arrows at my head and try to squash me with a car last night.' From the driver's seat, Mathew stared at me opened mouthed. 'We are on our way back to you. I know why the Old City Firm have been involved.'

'Oh, really? Do you mind if I put you on speaker phone? I am with Chief Inspector Quinn and a few others.'

At this stage I doubted it mattered how many people knew. 'Go ahead.'

I heard a buzz and then a brief moment of silence before the sound at the other end changed. 'Mrs Fisher,' said a new voice, 'this is Chief Inspector Quinn. I have several of my detectives with me. I understand there have been several attempts on your life recently.'

'You could say that. I gave DS Atwell a description of a man who has been following me. I take it you have had no luck in finding him.'

'That is correct, Mrs Fisher. I am diverting more men to the task now. You said something about the Old City Firm and why they are involved?'

He was prompting me to fill in a blank, so I did. 'It's not the Firm, just the top two guys. It transpires that Mrs Jeffries was in possession of some... sensitive pictures of the two of them from about thirty years ago.

Her office manager, Mathew Hughes, obtained them from her and used them as collateral for blackmail.'

'You're kidding,' scoffed Mike. Next to me I could feel the heat radiating off Mathew's cheeks.

I replied, 'I wish I was. I think Brevin and Drummond arranged Maggie's death as revenge for their embarrassment.'

'So, it was a professional hit,' stated the chief inspector. 'Where is Mr Hughes now?'

'Driving the car. We are on the M2 just passing Sittingbourne.'

'Very good. I want you to come directly to us, Mrs Fisher. Is that understood?' I thought about that for a moment. The local police had been ordered to hand over the Maggie Jeffries case, Superintendent Jenkins' team picking it up where they left off, but they could now claim they were pursuing the person attempting to murder me. In the course of their enquiries anything could happen such as accidentally arresting several members of the Old City Firm. It might burn a relationship somewhere but would still be a massive feather in the chief inspector's hat.

Mathew was on a ticking clock though and the Old City Firm were most likely poised to snatch, hurt or otherwise kill people tomorrow lunchtime if their demands were not met. Chief Inspector Quinn and his team wouldn't be able to reconcile this case that swiftly. I might be able to though.

Thinking fast, I said, 'We'll be there soon.' Then I disconnected and thought some more.

We were nearing the exit to take us to Maidstone, Mathew checking his rear view and clicking the turn signal on. I reached across and turned it off.

'What are you doing?' he asked.

I pursed my lips, trying to make my brain work faster. 'We're not going to Maidstone.'

Mathew frowned. 'But that police officer said...'

'I have a much better plan. Just keep driving for a bit, okay?' Our discussion took us past the exit, the next opportunity to leave the motorway not for several minutes and, if we kept going, the road we were on would take us right into central London.

I was going to roll the dice and gamble. It felt risky but I was sure it would eliminate any ambiguity. Using my phone, I searched for the Fox and Hounds pub at the end of Wopham Street and found a phone number for it. Steeling myself, I took a breath and pressed the button to connect me.

'Fox and Hounds,' a woman answered, probably the forty something barmaid with all the chest.

'Hello, this is Patricia Fisher calling for Jim Brevin or Ian Drummond.'

There was a pause before she asked, 'May I ask what this call is pertaining to?'

It was better than being told there was no one there by those names which I had considered a distinctly possible outcome. 'It is a private matter. I was with them yesterday. If you could please tell them who is calling and that I have something they want.'

The line went quiet and stayed that way for more than a minute. I began to think no one was coming to answer it but the sound of someone lifting the handset was obvious a moment before Jim Brevin's voice came on the line.

'Mrs Fisher?'

'Mr Brevin, thank you for taking the call. I am in possession of some photographs which I believe you would prefer to be in your hands.' He was quiet for so long that I thought he had gone. 'Mr Brevin?'

His gravelly voice came back suddenly. 'I'm going to transfer you to my office phone. The line will go silent until I pick it up at the other end. About thirty seconds, okay?' I told him yes and imagined his journey from the bar, where I assumed the barmaid had answered it, to his office way in the back. Thirty-three seconds later, his voice materialised once again. 'Still there, Mrs Fisher?'

'Yes.'

'I have you on speaker phone with my colleague. Please tell him what you just told me.'

'Mr Drummond, I have the photographs that Maggie took thirty years ago. I don't want them, and I don't want anyone else to get hurt, me especially. Please tell me what I need to do to get you to call off your attack dog. He's tried to kill me three times in the last twenty-four hours.'

I got another bout of silence, before Ian Drummond answered. 'We haven't set an attack dog on you, Mrs Fisher. We have no intention of causing you any harm at all.' I hadn't expected denial as an answer, but then realised they would never admit such a thing over a phone line. Before my brain could catch up and ask them the next question, he asked me one, 'Where is Mathew Hughes?'

Mathew stiffened and a small gasp of terror escaped his lips. 'I have him.' I looked directly into Mathew's eyes and held my finger to my lips so he knew to be quiet. 'You can have him, and the pictures. I just want to be left alone. Can we come to an arrangement?'

Jim Brevin asked, 'You plan to hand over Mathew Hughes and the photographs? What about the money?'

'I didn't take any money from you. That arrangement was with Mathew. I don't have a hundred grand to give you.'

'She's got a point,' said Ian.

'That she does,' replied Jim. 'It' a principle thing though. We didn't get here by letting a hundred grand slip through our fingers.'

'That's right, Jim, we didn't. The lady understands how these things work though. Let's not forget what she did to that bunch down in Miami. We get the photos and we get Mr Hughes. He will make a fine example of what happens when someone double crosses us.' Mathew whimpered quietly.

'Not to mention attempting to blackmail us,' added Jim.

'Good point, Jim,' said Ian.

I had laid the basis for my plan. They were on the hook, so to speak. Now I had to reel them in. 'I want to do this at Maggie's house.'

'Goodness, no, Mrs Fisher,' laughed Ian Drummond. 'Bring young Mr Hughes to us and we will take him off your hands.'

I expected that to be their reaction and was ready for it. 'I'm a fifty-three-year-old woman, Mr Drummond. I don't have him tied up in the trunk like one of your men probably would. I haven't beaten him to a pulp and were I to knock him out with something, I couldn't hope to shift his body. I need to lure him to you and that won't happen if I try to get him to London. He'll smell a rat straight away. I can get him to the countryside though; its familiar territory for him. Meet me at Maggie's in an hour. Can you do that?'

There was some discussion we could hear but not discern, the sound muffled as if a hand was across the phone. When they spoke again it was Jim Brevin addressing me, 'In an hour, Mrs Fisher. We won't be alone and if we smell the slightest hint of a trap, we'll vanish like smoke and then we really will set an attack dog on you. Don't do anything silly.' Then he hung up, the line going dead.

I slumped back into my seat not realising how tense I had been until the call ended.

'You're not really going to hand me over, are you?' Mathew asked, his voice barely more than a desperately frightened squeak.

I closed my eyes and exhaled deeply. 'No, Mathew. I'm going to topple their empire.' I could see the plan in my head. I just didn't know if I could pull it off. The difficult part was not involving the police. I expected them to demand it but it meant I was going to have to go in alone and use hope as a strategy, praying they wouldn't kill me to cover their tracks. I expected them to be technologically savvy and have equipment with them to detect recording devices. They would be that paranoid, I was sure, so I couldn't trap them into admitting crimes that would achieve a conviction which didn't leave me many options. The one it did leave me was unfavourable, especially for Mathew. I hadn't told him his part yet, but I didn't want to spoil the surprise.

In the quiet of the car, as the sun began to set, I sent a text message with detailed instructions and asked Mathew to take us both to Maggie's house.

Gambling with Lives

Maggie's house was as dark and deserted as it had been the last time I visited just a few days ago. I didn't have a key this time though. That ought to have been a problem, modern houses with modern windows and doors being so much harder to break into, but I knew where she kept the spare. She and I had been friends for most of five decades, since we went to school together as little girls, so she didn't keep much from me. She kept the fact that she was sleeping with my husband from me, but on balance that was probably all.

The key was under the rock by the window at the corner of the east oast as it always was, and I had the door open moments after arriving. Mathew parked his car in full view at the front of the house so anyone approaching would know we were there, and we turned on a whole bunch of lights to illuminate the house.

He was nervous and agitated, a natural reaction given what we were about to do. Not that I had told him what we were about to do. In fact, I lied through my teeth to the poor young man. It was necessary; he would never go through with my plan if I revealed it. I told him he was going to hide in a closet near the front door. They would come in and I would send him a text message from my pocket so he could slip out and escape. The police were coming, I assured him, and he believed every word. He even thanked me for my help and for my bravery because I was sticking around inside the house with the gangsters as the police swarmed in to arrest them all.

No such thing was going to happen because they had no crime to arrest them for. Not yet at least. My plan was going to resolve that.

They arrived five minutes after us, three black Mercedes sedans crunching over the gravel as they made their way up toward the house.

Loyal lieutenants exited the car first, dressed in black and looking like professional security guards in neat suits with curly wires running up to their left ears. Two men opened the rear doors on the middle of the three cars so Brevin and Drummond could exit. I was outnumbered a dozen to one. It was just me, since Mathew was securely tucked away in the walk-in closet by the door.

The front door was open so they could see me standing inside. I turned away and walked into the lounge as they began to approach, sending a quick text message and putting my phone away before they got to me. No words were exchanged, the first two men advancing with an electronic box which they carried between them. They placed it on the floor and pressed a button before folding out a screen from one side. Several men crowded around the screen while yet another man advanced on me carrying a small black box from which a thin wand ran on an even thinner wire.

As they did so, Jim Brevin asked, 'Are you quite alright, Mrs Fisher? You look a little worse for wear.'

I looked down at my clothes. They were ripped and dirty, the result of throwing myself out of the car. I had soot on my hands and bits of sticking plaster on my knuckles, chin and both ears. 'I have had a tough day.'

'She's clean,' the man with the wand thing announced after a few seconds of wafting it around me.

'The house is clean,' announced one of the men standing by the large box on the floor. 'No devices at all.'

Jim Brevin nodded his head. 'Well done, Mrs Fisher. I have to say I thought you would disappoint me and try something foolish like informing the police and filling this place with recording devices.'

'Now where's Mr Hughes,' demanded Ian Drummond, his mouth a sneer. He wanted to get on with the murdery part of the evening.

'In a moment, Mr Drummond, if you please. There are no devices here, you are quite safe. I am severely outnumbered and have no weapons. This exchange will take just a few moments, but I hoped to extend it just a few seconds by asking you about Maggie and why she had to die.'

Drummond, his patience boiling over, took a pace toward me, stopping only when Brevin placed an arm in his way. 'The lady makes a fair request, Ian,' he pointed out. 'However, the problem with your request, Mrs Fisher, is that we have already answered you: We didn't kill her. Even without recording equipment here to incriminate ourselves, we still didn't kill her. No matter what way the question gets asked or if you use truth serum. We still didn't kill her. And, to be very clear, we didn't hire someone else to do it for us.'

'We killed plenty of other people,' chipped in Ian.

'Yes, Ian. But we didn't kill, Maggie.'

'That's right, Jim. We didn't. She was an old friend.'

Everything about the case and the fact that I still couldn't work out who had killed Maggie was really beginning to annoy me. The time of death, the evidence generally told me that these two gangsters hadn't killed her. But the photographs, the constant attempts on my life, all told a different story. I just couldn't make sense of it. Someone had killed Maggie. They took a gun and placed it next to her temple before pulling the trigger. That sort of thing isn't easy to do. If I accepted that the Old City Firm were not responsible, then who could I blame? I was coming completely full circle for the second time.

Drummond was still pushing against his partner to get to me which meant I had more pressing concerns than identifying Maggie's killer right now. I fished in my handbag to retrieve the photographs. 'Here,' I said, handing them over.

'Where's Hughes?' growled Drummond.

'He's in the closet by the front door.'

It was quiet enough in the house for Mathew to hear me speaking so he heard me give him up. As everyone swivelled around to look back toward the front door, we heard the sound of him bursting from his hiding place and trying to escape. He didn't get far, the Old City Firm left guards outside by the cars as I expected they would. My plan had never been to let Mathew escape. In fact my plan depended on his capture.

From outside, where three men were manhandling Mathew into the boot of the middle car, his voice carried across the quiet evening air, 'How could you?' The terror and betrayal in his voice cut right through me.

'Cooee!' My heart froze in my chest.

All the faces in the room stared at me, their eyes accusing.

'Cooee,' Mavis the busybody strolled in. The front door had been abandoned as the men chased Mathew outside. 'I saw all the lights on and thought I would just pop in to introduce myself. Are you the new neighbours?'

'Mavis, get out of here,' I squeaked.

Jim Brevin crossed the room with his arms open in welcome. 'Mavis, is it? Come in, come in.' Then, just as he got to her, he produced a stiletto blade and held it to her throat. One of his men grabbed her from behind to pin her arms as Jim's face swung back to stare at me. 'What is this, Mrs

Fisher? You were so close to getting off the hook. Do you know how often Ian and I let people go?'

'It's not often,' answered Ian. 'Is she wearing a wire?'

'An underwire?' squawked Mavis. 'Why are you asking about my bra? Is this one of those strange fetish parties?'

'Nah, she's clean, boss,' answered the man holding her as he frisked her all over with one hand.

'Here, get off me, young man,' Mavis demanded. 'Or take me somewhere private at least.'

I rolled my eyes. It had to be Mavis. I was seconds from concluding the whole affair and she ruined it by sticking her busybody nose in. Even if we lived through this, she would spend the next few years telling everyone she interrupted me having some kind of sordid gang sex party at a dead woman's house. She wouldn't care that it wasn't true, good gossip rarely is.

'What now, Ian?' asked Jim.

Ian pursed his lips. 'We take them all. Easier to dispose of at our facility.'

An arm looped around my waist from behind and a hand clamped over my mouth. I tried to kick and scream and bite the hand over my mouth, but he was far too strong and his hands far too big. He had his thumb looped over the bridge of my nose and two fingers under my chin, forcing my mouth shut as if he had been trained in how to kidnap a woman. A second man moved in to grab my legs.

Through panic-stricken eyes, I could see Mavis getting the same treatment a few yards ahead of me. The men carrying me followed her out of the house and down the steps where they split off to take me to the rear car as Mavis was taken to the front.

This wasn't the plan!

I was supposed to stay in the house as they all left with Mathew. The next part of the plan was dangerous enough without me being in the boot of the car.

Still struggling as they carried me, I glimpsed the boot lid just before they swung me backward. That they were going to throw me in only occurred to me just as my body weight reached the apex of the backswing and started toward the car.

They let go, allowing me to fly for a half second before I crashed into the unforgiving steel of the boot. If I didn't have enough bruises already, here were a few more to add to them.

The boot lid slammed down, shutting off all light and plunging me into darkness. It was a terrifying experience; yet another one to add to my list. Thunking sounds from the doors shutting and a settling of the suspension told me they were getting in the car. The engine started and the sensation of moving let me know we were on our way.

At this point, I was either going to get taken to London and fed to the fishes in the Thames or the neatly organised plan was going to work, and I would be rescued along with Mavis and Mathew. The third option, and the one I currently thought most likely, was that the road block and trap at each end of the village the Old City Firm were now driving into would result in a shootout with police marksmen and I would get riddled with bullet holes.

The text message I sent in the car was to DS Atwell. I instructed him to set the roadblocks and to be swift about it, getting everything in place once I gave the signal, which I did with a second text message the moment they arrived.

The first message told the police that the Old City Firm were coming to the village and would be leaving with a kidnap victim. I was gambling with Mathew's life, my reasoning being that they would kill him later where they felt safe to do so, not at Maggie's house. It was most definitely a gamble but one I felt, on balance of probabilities, was safe to take. It had proven correct, but the plan then got scuppered by Mavis poking her nose in.

So, now I was in the boot of a car and any second now a police trap was going to be sprung on the three-car convoy of gangsters. Would Chief Inspector Quinn have enough foresight to instruct his marksmen to aim clear of the boot space? Would they even be able to? What about ricochets?

In the darkness of the boot, I could hear muffled voices coming through from the car's interior, then the sound of someone in the road using a loud hailer and yelling instructions. The car screeched to a stop, reversed direction and shot backwards, the driver performing a handbrake turn in reverse to make his getaway. The police were prepared for that though, the sound of tyres bursting reached my ears just before I felt the car go out of control. I was being bounced and thrown around like a cat in a tumble dryer, but the final slam and crunch as the car came to a halt popped the boot letting starlight spill in. It also bounced me hard enough to almost throw me out. I was going to be so sore the next few days, but I had an escape route now and needed to take it no matter how I felt.

The shocking noise of shots being exchanged, intermingled with barked orders from the police, punctuated the night. Grasping the edge of the boot, I hauled myself up and over it to tumble out onto the ground outside. It was damp but that was the least of my worries. Mostly my head was filled with worry for Mavis and especially Mathew, who I had lied to so I could get this far. How would I forgive myself if he got killed tonight?

The men in black suits were all bundling out of the car, steam rising from its bonnet where it had left the road on unusable tyres and crashed into a tree. Fifty yards behind us in the road was one of those stinger things with all the spikes. I couldn't see much, cowering behind and under the tail end of the car as I was, but I saw the approaching boots coming in on every side and heard the barked orders to drop their weapons.

A shout of, 'Get stuffed, copper,' preceded a hail of bullets as presumably, one of the gangsters pulled his gun and the armed police cut him down. A body crashed to the ground next to me, his eyes imploring me to help him as life leaked from his chest.

I curled into a ball and prayed it would stop soon.

When a hand touched my shoulder, I screamed.

'Patricia.' The hand was tapping my shoulder. 'Patricia, it's over.' I knew the voice, I realised. It was Mike Atwell, the friendly local detective sergeant. Uncurling my head to take a peek, I saw him kneeling on the damp ground to peer under the car at me. 'It's over, you're safe,' he promised me.

'Mavis and Mathew?' I asked, fearing what he might tell me.

'Both shaken but they are not hurt.'

The news washed through me and brought with it a wave of exhaustion. Even though I was already on the ground, my whole body sagged and flopped, the terrible anxiety leaving me as a crashing sense of relief made me want to cry.

Five minutes later, I was sitting on the back step of an ambulance with a blanket around me and a cup of tea in my hands. Inside, Mavis was being treated for a suspected mild heart attack which turned out to be indigestion, the pain in her chest dissipating when she farted loudly to the surprise of all within earshot.

'Oh, that's much better,' she announced and followed it up with another.

I clambered onto still shaky legs and tottered over to where DS Atwell was conversing with two officers in uniform. 'Ah, Mrs Fisher, this is Chief Inspector Quinn,' DS Atwell introduced his superior. The chief inspector was a lean man of about forty, who looked like an endurance athlete, someone who took part in ultra-marathons perhaps. He was a shade over six feet tall and was local, if his accent was anything to go by. His nose bore a small scar which suggested it might have an interesting story but could just as easily have been from a childhood accident.

Chief Inspector Quinn was coordinating the mop up. Many of the Old City Firm had been injured, two had been killed when they returned fire but all those still alive were under arrest and on their way to jail soon. Most of them were still on the road as they waited for another prisoner van to arrive.

I didn't see him at first, his head was down, but when he called my name, I turned to see Jim Brevin looking up at me with a smug smile. 'Well played, Mrs Fisher,' he congratulated me, making it sound genuine. 'Well done. Watch your back though, won't you now. There's a lot more of my boys still out there than you see before you tonight and how sure are you that they will manage to make a conviction stick?'

Chief Inspector Quinn answered him. 'You were caught in possession of illegal firearms and with three kidnapped persons in the boots of your cars. You'll never walk free again, man. Delude yourself if you wish, but you can have my personal guarantee of life imprisonment.'

Brevin continued to smile at me, never once breaking eye contact as they lifted him to his feet and took him away. Whether his threats were idle or not, they would keep me awake at night for a while.

People from the village had turned out to see what all the noise and flashing lights were for, a small but growing crowd forming behind the police line. I spotted Charlie among the crowd and waved to him. He waved back, acknowledging that he had seen me.

'Chief Inspector?'

'Yes?'

'Am I free to go?'

'Go, Mrs Fisher? You look like the only place you should be going is the hospital. Haven't you been in two car crashes so far today?' I nodded, trying not to laugh at the daft irony of my life because it would hurt too much. 'I will require a full statement, Mrs Fisher, but that can wait until tomorrow. Would you like to come to the station? Or shall I send someone to your house.'

I was about to say I would come to them, but my memory caught up with me. 'I don't have a car. Can you send someone, please?'

He nodded. 'Of course. Someone will be along at 1400hrs sharp.'

I translated that in my head to two o'clock. 'Super. Good luck with the rest of it.' He mumbled a good evening to my back as I walked away. I was desperate to get home to see Anna. I also wanted to find a large glass of gin and go for a swim in it, but there was something else I needed to do first.

Mathew had been treated for shock and was waiting to be taken to hospital. I knew that much from asking Mike about him earlier. There was a pressing need to apologise for using him as human bait and figured I might never get another chance. I found him in the back of the ambulance just as they were about to shut the door and leave.

'You've got one minute,' said the paramedic as he stepped outside to give me space.

Mathew looked up at me from the gurney. He was all strapped in for transport and had a bandage around his head. 'I hit it getting out of the car,' he explained when he saw me looking at it. I started to speak but he cut across me. 'I want to thank you, Mrs Fisher. What you did was so clever. I feel I should scream at you for not telling me your plan, but I wouldn't have been brave enough to go through with it if you had. You caught them all, just like you said you would. Lured them in and let them commit a crime they can't come back from. I'm free.'

'Yes,' I agreed. 'You're free. You might need to consider your position at the firm though. Not that it is any of my business, but I doubt you will be able to keep the embezzlement a secret now.'

'No,' he agreed sadly. 'No, that had occurred to me. I think I need to move back home with mum and dad and think about what I want to do next.' He started fidgeting under the blanket they had over him. It was under the straps, so he had to wriggle around a bit to get his right arm free. 'Here,' he said, finally lifting his arm clear. In his hand was the key to the Aston Martin. 'The lease is paid up to the end of the month. Can you keep hold of it for me? I know I have no right to ask any favours, but I really don't need it and I know you don't have a car at the moment. Say no if it is an inconvenience.'

A smile fluttered across my face as my hand closed around the key. I didn't have to keep it for long. Heck I couldn't afford to, but I would enjoy the couple of weeks I had with it while I looked for my next car. 'Thank you, Mathew.'

'I'll send over the lease details so you can return it.'

The ambulance door opened again. 'Time's up. We really need to get this one to the hospital.' The paramedic looked at me. 'You look like you could do with being checked over too, do you want to come with us?'

I shook my head and stood up. 'No, thank you.' With a final pat on Mathew's leg, I stepped back outside and wandered over to the police line where the crowd of villagers had formed. I didn't see Charlie anymore, but I didn't look all that hard for him either. The crowd parted to let me through, people staring as I passed between them, but no one tried to stop me with questions. I walked on stiff legs, the aches and pains in my body seeming to multiply with every step as I made my way back almost a mile to Maggie's house.

I got the car and went home.

Working It Out

The following morning, I awoke late, the numbing effect of the five G&Ts from last night having finally worn off. Charlie was home when I got there, asking dozens of questions about the fantastic car I arrived in; he saw it through the kitchen window as I pulled up and had to come out to help me put the roof up. He also had questions about the police and the gangsters and who Maggie's killer was.

The final question proved to be a problem because I still didn't know. I couldn't name a mystery I had come across that was this complex before. From the outset, it looked as if Maggie had involved herself in nefarious dealing and come a cropper because of them. She hadn't though. The embezzling, the loan sharking, the blackmail, she hadn't been aware of any of it. The only part she had played was to take pictures thirty years ago and then reveal their existence to the wrong person. According to Brevin and Drummond, who remained adamant on this point; they hadn't killed her either directly or by ordering her murder.

So, who had? The man with no neck, after having three solid goes at trying to kill me, hadn't been found by the police and hadn't tried again for twelve hours now. The Old City Firm boys denied sending him too. One might want to argue that I couldn't trust a word they said, but the thing is, I did. I believed them when they said they didn't kill Maggie and that she was an old friend. I believed them when they told me they didn't send the man with no neck. So, who was he and why was he so desperate to kill me? Was he Maggie's killer also?

Getting out of bed, I put my foot in something damp and lifted it again. I stared at it curiously until my head got into gear and told me what I was looking at.

Anna's waters had broken!

I found her in her bed. It was a bit icky. She looked ready for the event and licked my nose when I got close enough. Moving fast despite my aching body, I threw on clothes, lifted the whole bed, kicked the door open and rushed downstairs.

'Charlie!'

'What?' echoed back through the house. I put the bed and dog on the carpet in the living room near the couch, trying to keep my pulse from racing as I began to panic about what I needed to do to help her. Charlie's voice drifted through as he came to find me, 'Patricia I know I didn't put up a fight when you needed to stay here for a couple of days, but this is becoming an inconvenience.' He stopped in the doorway to the living room when he spotted me. 'What's happening?'

'Anna is having her puppies,' I told him, my voice trembling with excitement and anxiousness.

'Not on my couch, she isn't,' he snapped.

'She's not on...' I swung back around from addressing Charlie to see that Anna had indeed climbed onto the couch and was making a nest to settle into.

Charlie moved to pick her up and she growled in warning and then snapped at him when he didn't back away.

I tapped him on the shoulder. 'I think perhaps you should leave her to get on with it.'

'It's a suede couch, Patricia,' he whined.

'I know, Charlie,' I was already leaving the room to look for towels and a small bowl I could put water in so she wouldn't have to move if she got thirsty. 'I bought it.'

Another growl and snap from Anna told me Charlie had foolishly tried again. I heard him grumble the words, 'With my money,' under his breath as he retreated.

Ignoring him, I gathered the bits I wanted and settled on the carpet in front of the sofa to be with her, cooing and chatting away to her brainlessly. She didn't pay me much attention and I seemed entirely surplus to requirement, so when my back started to get sore, I stood up and went to the dining table. There, I grabbed a pad and a pen and had yet another go at assembling the clues pertaining to Maggie's murder.

Before I could write the first word, a knock at the door interrupted me, Charlie opening the door a moment later to let Emily the house cleaner in. I didn't think she worked Saturdays, most cleaners don't, but here she was in her gear and ready to go. Perhaps Charlie had something specific for her to do.

I went back to the pad and started writing notes. My subset of suspects contained the man with no neck and no one else. He was only in there because I didn't know who he was and had no explanation for his presence in the village. There was no one else. I scratched my head. I was a terrible detective. I moved in my chair and groaned when almost every part of my body protested. I needed tea.

In the kitchen, I filled the kettle and set it to boil, popping my head back through the door to check on Anna. She seemed comfortable enough on the couch and I certainly wasn't going to move her despite Charlie's protests. I would sooner buy him a new couch, and besides, her waters had already broken upstairs; how much more mess could she make?

I felt bad that I never managed to get to a vet with her; it made me feel like a bad doggy mum. She was taking it all in her stride though, somehow knowing exactly what to do without needing a midwife or a delivery suite or half a dozen books to read on the subject.

When the kettle clicked off, I made a cup of tea, leaving her to it. It wasn't in my nature to hold a grudge against Charlie, so I called through the house to him, 'Charlie, I'm making tea, do you want one?' I got no answer, so I tried again and when I still got no answer, I made him one anyway. He would either want it or he wouldn't. Taking the teabags out a minute later I deposited them in the kitchen waste bin under the sink and rinsed the spoon and that was when I spotted it.

Across the driveway, Emily's grey car was tucked against a hedge, but I could see the front bumper and the scuff mark on it. I was squinting my eyes to better make out the colour of the paint scraped onto it, but I knew if I went outside, I would find out it was red.

Suddenly it all fell into place. Emily had killed Maggie. She had a key to her house and could walk up to her without Maggie paying her any attention at all. I could see it all in my head. Emily would always be carrying cleaning things about with her. Maybe even in a bucket so she walked up to Maggie, or maybe even behind her, pulled a gun from the bucket and shot her in the head. It was cold and dispassionate which had thrown me because it looked and felt like an execution, not a crime of passion.

I knew that when I looked into it, I would discover some terrible secret like Emily's husband had slept with Maggie and she had taken her revenge. I reached for my phone.

'Don't do that, please,' the sudden voice in the quiet house made me jump and I spun around to find Emily standing behind me. She blocked the kitchen door and had a gun in her hand.

'Emily,' I stuttered. 'What's going on?'

She tilted her head slightly, a disappointed look crossing her face. 'I knew you would work it out. That's why I kept trying to kill you. It seemed to me to be the simplest and cleanest solution. I was a champion archer, you know. I couldn't believe it when you ducked my first shot and then the second. I felt certain you would get burned up in the car, but you survived that too. Oh, sure there would then be another investigation but the police seemed so convinced by my waterworks last time, and so taken with the idea that Maggie's death could be connected to organised crime, I figure I can manage to fool them again.' She moved around to get a better angle, keeping the gun on me the whole time. 'It was so easy to make it look like an execution. I got the idea from a murder mystery book you know. The detective caught the killer because the crime was frenzied, not cold and calculating. I just switched it around.'

There were knives in a block to my right. If I edged around just a bit, looking terrified and as if I was trying to get away, maybe I could snag one and throw it at her. It wasn't much against a gun, but I wasn't going to find a gun anywhere. Suddenly, a thought occurred to me. 'Where's Charlie?'

She laughed at me, a scoffing noise of derision. 'That cheating scumbag. Yet another man to fall into her spider's web. You should be thanking me.' I felt a rush of panic. Had she killed him already? Seeing my concern, she said, 'I haven't done it yet. I just knocked him out for now. I'm glad you survived my attempts to kill you actually, this is much neater. The two of you are going to have a bit of a fight and you will get killed by him in a fit of rage. Killed by the same weapon as the one which killed Maggie, his former lover and the woman who ruined his marriage. He'll leave a lovely note about how he thought killing her to get her out of the way might help him to win you back but when you refused to return to him, he killed you and then took his own life.'

I wanted to say that she was mad, but in all honesty, I thought she was going to get away with it. It would all be so neat. Shoot me, then shoot him, carefully making sure to explode the part of his skull where she had knocked him out so there was no evidence of it to find.

I took a step toward the knife block, a faked stumble as if I was fainting and then catching myself. She shot a hole in the sink.

I screamed and darted back the way I had come, almost knocking over the cups of tea in my haste.

'Nice try,' she sneered. 'I was in the Army; I can shoot you in the eye from here.' She studied me curiously. 'I have to say I expected you to work it out long before this. Patricia Fisher the super sleuth. All those adventures just to get killed by your husband. Aren't you going to ask me why?'

'Go on then, tell me why.'

She made a big show of spreading her arms to get the big explanation going, breaking into gesticulations as I hoped she would. 'Well...'

She saw me move, but the first cup of steaming hot tea was already flying toward her. Unbelievably, my aim was true, the cup and its contents flying across the room at her head. She fired another shot, the sound loud enough for me to feel it even though I was sure it hadn't hit me.

The cup hit the wall where her head had been, smashing instantly to shower her in pieces of crockery and hot liquid. I'm certain she would have screamed in protest if the second cup, aimed a foot and a half lower, hadn't hit her in the face.

I was beyond terrified at this point, running across the room to get to her even though every nerve in my body wanted me to run the other way.

She was stunned and momentarily blinded by the scalding hot liquid but my hope that the mug of tea might just knock her out was dashed completely. She was coming out of her crouch and raising the gun as I closed with her. I had no more weapons; the knife block had seemed to be too far away, so with just my battered and bruised body, I slammed into her, knocking her over backwards as I scrambled for the gun.

She was still in the kitchen doorway, so tumbled backward with me on top of her, both of us trying to get the better grip on the other. She was half my age and stronger than me. If the fight went on, I would simply lose, so it was with great relief that I saw her gun hand hit the skirting board at a terrible angle, snapping her wrist with an audible crack as my hand pushed her wrist downward. The gun flew free as she bellowed in pain and rage. That ought to have been the end of the fight but she wasn't done. Like some ancient warrior, she refused to give up, punching the side of my head as I tried to go for the gun. I had to fight my way off her, sliding over her face while she tried to bite me. The gun was six feet away, lying on the carpet tantalisingly begging me to pick it up. She snagged my legs though, squirming around despite the broken arm to get out from under me. Then, with a kick to my middle, she was on top and getting up. She was going to get to the gun first and there was nothing I could do about it. I slipped on the carpet in my haste to propel myself forward, landing painfully and jarring my knees. Glancing along the hallway, I saw that I was beaten. I couldn't possibly stop her now; she was two feet from the gun and already bending down to pick it up.

It was because I looked that I saw what happened next.

A shadow crossed in front of her where the front door joined the hallway running through the downstairs of the house. The shadow then became a leg and then a whole body as the man with no neck stepped into the hallway, assessed what he was seeing in a heartbeat, and hit Emily with his briefcase.

She slumped to the floor, tried to get up once and then collapsed unconscious.

My heartrate was through the roof from all the adrenalin and exertion but the appearance of the man who had been tracking me for the last few days was the final straw. I started crying, unable to hold in the desperate panic I felt. It had been Emily trying to kill me this week, not this man, at least that was what I now believed, but he was here to finish me off and I had no fight left in me.

Watching from the floor, as he checked Emily's pulse, secured the gun and started along the hallway toward me, I breathlessly managed, 'Just tell me who sent you. I need to know which group ordered my execution, please!' Was it the Boris's Russian friends? The Capriones? Could it be Prince Zebrahim reaching out from jail to get me? Maybe it was the terrorists from East Houptiou. They waited until I got home and would be less well protected, biding their time but getting me, nevertheless. Maybe he wouldn't tell me, and I would never know.

His feet came closer and closer, looking huge from where I lay helpless on the carpet. Then he stopped right by my head. 'Execution, Mrs Fisher? Whatever are you talking about? Might I give you a hand up? Are you quite alright?'

Now I was confused. I twisted my head around so I could see his face. His accent was Surrey or perhaps Hampshire, definitely somewhere south but delivered with a distinct twang of well-bred. His left hand was extended down to help me up.

As I took it, my hand tiny inside his huge mitt, he said, 'My name is Morris Worthington. I am the senior partner of Worthington,

Worthington, Worthington, and Smythe. I am tasked with ensuring a gift from the Maharaja of Zangrabar is delivered in person.'

But It's Not My Birthday

I swear I almost fainted with relief when my brain finally caught up and accepted that I wasn't about to die. However, once the room stopped swimming, I remembered Charlie and Anna. As I let go of Morris's hand and started running through the house he called after me, 'Mrs Fisher, what should I do with the gun? And the injured lady?'

As I stuck my head through a door, failed to find Charlie and moved on, I yelled back. 'Call the police. And if she comes around, don't give her the gun back. Feel completely free to shoot her with it, in fact.'

He said something which sounded like, 'Goodness,' but I was hitting the stairs by then, running up them to search the upper floor. I eventually found Charlie on our marital bed. He had a lump the size and shape of a golf ball protruding from the back of his skull. I didn't know or care what she had hit him with because he was alive and breathing and his pulse felt normal. Relief washed through me like a wave of dizziness, forcing me to steady myself on the bed.

I shook him. 'Wake up, Charlie.' No response. More effort and volume the next time. 'Wake up, Charlie!' Still no response, so I grabbed the cup of water from the bedside table, picked my aiming mark, and threw it at him.

He came awake pretty fast then, sitting up too quickly only to duck down again as his head pounded in protest. 'Oh, my lord, what happened. Did you hit me with something, Patricia?'

'Emily is the killer, dummy. She hit you and planned to kill the both of us to cover her tracks. You were to be framed as Maggie's killer and I was to be your second victim, killed because I refused to take you back.'

'What?' he asked, his pathetic brain overloaded by my explanation.

I hooked an arm under his. 'Come on. Let's get you downstairs. I need to get an ambulance here. You might have a concussion.'

Slowly, I manoeuvred him downstairs and into an armchair across from Anna. He settled into it and then jumped out of his skin as he saw Morris looming in the doorway that led in from the kitchen. To be fair, Morris filled the doorway almost completely top to bottom and he was still holding the gun.

'It's okay,' I assured Charlie with a pat on his arm. 'He's with me. I'll get you some ice for your head.'

From the doorway, Morris said, 'The police are on their way, Mrs Fisher. Shall I call an ambulance also?'

'Yes, please, Mr Worthington. That would be most helpful.' I was about to go for ice when I spotted Anna. She was licking something, and when I looked, it moved. There was a puppy tucked under her chin. I fell to my knees in front of the couch. 'Oh, Anna, you clever little girl,' I was gushing, and once again my eyes were filling up with tears. Amid all the crazy carnage, murder, and mayhem, my little Dachshund had produced something perfect.

Behind me, Charlie asked, 'Patricia why is my groin wet?' The answer to that particular question was that I had elected to throw the glass of water at his trousers instead of his head. I figured it would get the same result at his end, but I would enjoy it more.

I didn't bother to answer him, choosing instead to kiss Anna on top of her head before leaving her to get the ice. When I came back, there was a second puppy. By the time the police and the ambulance arrived fifteen minutes later there were four. My little dog produced four perfect puppies. I guess they were Dachshund Corgi crosses, but they looked like Dachshunds to me. Whatever they were, they were gorgeous little balls of fur, each of them feeding on mummy as she lay exhausted on her side. I fed her pieces of dog meat with a teaspoon, cooing at her the whole time and ignoring everyone around me as they fussed and tried to ask me questions.

When eventually I tore myself away from the couch, I found DS Atwell in my kitchen with Chief Inspector Quinn. 'I hadn't expected to see you again so soon, Mrs Fisher,' the senior policeman commented.

'Yes,' I agreed.

'Are you hurt?' he asked, concern, whether faked or sincere, filled his face.

'I'm fine. A few more bruises and scrapes. Nothing to get excited about.'

He nodded as I spoke. 'Good, Mrs Fisher. I'm glad to hear it. I would like one of my officers to take a preliminary statement from you and I will have to leave a team here to make sure we have all the evidence. It appears to be an open and shut case this time though. Conviction will be easy, since she already confessed.'

'Oh?' No one had told me. 'Did she say why she killed Maggie?'

'Her brother,' the chief Inspector told me. 'He was a gardener here some time ago. Mrs Jeffries, according to Emily Walker, seduced him and ruined his life. She used him as a plaything and rejected him when he developed feelings for her. He wasn't able to get over it and she sacked him from the job as gardener when he became a nuisance. He committed suicide a few weeks ago and Miss Walker blames Mrs Jeffries.'

A sad circumstance all around.

CI Quinn continued, 'She planned the whole thing. The gun was hers, a trophy she brought back from Iraq a few years ago. She knew the house and gardens well enough to know only the front door was being videoed, so she came in through the woodland behind the house, left a door unlocked when she was there to clean earlier that day. She even confessed to the multiple attempts on your life. She was a childhood archery champion apparently.'

DS Atwell said, 'We identified the make and model of the paint on the car that almost killed you on Thursday night. It came from a Renault Clio, the same car that Miss Walker drives.'

'Really?' I replied, my voice dripping with sarcasm. 'That information would have been a little more useful a day ago.'

'Better late than never,' he smiled.

We talked for a few minutes until he handed me off to a constable who introduced himself as PC Hardacre. I insisted that we conduct the statement taking portion of this morning's adventure in Charlie's living room where Anna was still nursing her four puppies. I gently stroked her head and cooed at her between answering his questions.

When that was finally complete and he had thanked me and confirmed I was free to go, I turned my attention toward the very patient and very persistent Mr Morris Worthington. He was sitting at the dining table in the dining room working on a laptop computer. His briefcase was closed and placed neatly next to his chair. Because of his size, everything in the room looked undersized like one of those rooms at a fun house where the walls are at an angle so people at the far end look really tall. His calves were so long his knees barely fit beneath the table and he made the chair look like it was one taken from a kindergarten. He wasn't a contract killer or a henchman though, he was a lawyer who was born tall and liked the gym.

'Mr Worthington, thank you so much for saving me earlier.' Shamefully I had forgotten to thank him until now.

He stopped typing, closed his laptop and turned toward me. The chair creaked dangerously. 'Think nothing of it, Mrs Fisher.'

I shook my head. 'I am forever in your debt, Mr Worthington. She would most surely have killed me if you had not intervened when you did.'

He didn't argue. Instead, he said, 'Then I am glad she did not succeed. It would have made my job far more complicated.'

I took a seat at the dining table, finally able to indulge my curiosity about the man and his task. 'Yes, you said you have a gift from the Maharaja of Zangrabar? How long have you been tracking me?'

Mr Worthington flipped his eyebrows in amusement. 'Only since you returned to England. I waited at the royal suites' exit onto the quayside at Southampton but managed somehow to miss you there.' I remembered choosing to leave by the standard exit. 'My firm was contacted only three weeks ago with very specific instructions. I have to say that it caused a great flurry of work for us but that we have been only too happy to fulfil the Maharaja's desires.'

The young king had sent a gift for me. I imagined it would be a piece of extravagant jewellery or something equally expensive and unnecessary. In my head, Mr Worthington was about to produce a pair of ruby earrings worth a million pounds. They would solve all my financial concerns about buying a house for myself and replacing my car, but of course they wouldn't at all because I would never be able to sell them: who sells a gift from a king the moment they get it?

I couldn't bear to wait any longer, the suspense was killing me, and my nerves were already too frazzled for me to hold off the gin for much longer: I was going to the post office to buy a bottle as soon as Mr Worthington departed. 'What has he sent me?' I asked, my voice a hushed breath of anticipation.

In response, he lifted the briefcase, placed it on the table, opened both the snaps with a click, but then instead of taking out what the Maharaja had sent me, he picked up his laptop and placed it inside. The lid closed again, and I found myself confused as to what was now happening when he started to extricate himself from the table to get up. 'It would be better to show you, Mrs Fisher.'

'It would?' I was still sitting but he extended his hand to help me up again and I wondered, as I followed him from the dining room, if his hand had been to get me moving because his patience was perhaps invisibly wearing thin. I couldn't blame him if that was the case. I had given him the run around for three days, actively avoiding him and putting barriers in his path.

Outside, he walked to his large Jaguar sedan and opened the rear door for me. Once again holding out his hand to help me in. 'Where are we going?' I asked.

'It is not far, Mrs Fisher.' His cryptic reply set my nerves on edge as if I were once again in danger and about to be led into a trap. Seeing my expression in his rear-view mirror, he tried to reassure me. 'You are without a vehicle now, is that correct, Mrs Fisher?'

'Sort of. It caught fire. I have… a loaner for now.' I was unreasonably upset about my Ford's demise. It was mechanically unsound, ten years old and worth almost nothing. It was all I had though and now I had to take more money from the pot designated for house buying so I could replace it. The Aston Martin would be fun for a short time but also meant whatever I got next would be rubbish by comparison.

From the driver's seat, Mr Worthington said with confidence, 'I believe that situation is about to be resolved.'

My eyebrows climbed my head. 'He bought me a car?'

'It is better if I show you, Mrs Fisher.'

Now my head was crammed with images of swanky cars; Ferraris or Lamborghinis, other makes of supercars that someone like the Maharaja wouldn't think twice about buying. It would be completely inappropriate for me and I would have to sell it. What was a Ferrari worth, I wondered?

He drove for a few minutes only. His route taking us through the village of East Malling and into West Malling but as we reached West Malling High Street and turned up toward Tonbridge, he indicated and turned left. There was nothing down this road to my knowledge except the park. He continued for half a mile, passing the park itself before indicating again and taking a right turn. Up a slight incline he then turned left once more but was now entering someone's drive. Not like a normal drive which is ten yards long if your house is set well back from the road, this one was more like a road, but as we went along it, I began to see a house through the trees.

'Who lives here?' I asked.

Once again, I got his cryptic response, 'It is better if I show you, Mrs Fisher.'

I could not claim that I felt relaxed, but I was no longer hovering above the seat with my nerves telling me I was being driven to my death and a shallow grave in the woods. The car followed the driveway as it swung around and lined up on the house. I call it a house, but in reality, it was far too grand for such a mediocre title. A large door sat dead centre with three large sash windows each side so either the rooms were huge or there were a lot of rooms. We were heading directly for it, the driveway lined up on the front door so I couldn't tell how deep the building was though I was willing to bet it was at least as deep as it was wide. The entire façade was rendered and painted bright white, three columns either side of the front door supported a wide balcony above it.

It was a splendid property and in thinking that I realised that it must be the Maharaja's England residence. It screamed opulence. 'Is this the Maharaja's house?' I asked, confident that I had worked it out and wondering if he was here to give me his gift in person.

'Yes, Mrs Fisher.' I sat back in my chair, pleased that I was going to see the young king again. 'And no.' Mr Worthington concluded, confusing me once again. Seeing my brow furrow, he finally tried to put me out of my misery as he stopped the car. 'This is now your house, Mrs Fisher.'

I heard exactly what he said, yet I couldn't make any sense of his words. How could this be my house? 'But,' I managed to say one word as I stared at Mr Worthington and waited for the unfair punchline to come. He smiled at me over his shoulder, his head and body turned in his seat to meet my eyes. 'But,' I said again.

Mr Worthington opened his door and got out, walking slowly around the car to open my door as well. Once again, he offered his hand to help me get out. I accepted it, sliding around and out with my knees together, trying to be ladylike though my clothes looked like I had been fighting in them. As I stood up, he opened his left hand to let a set of keys dangle from them.

'My instructions were to find you as you departed the Aurelia, Mrs Fisher. I apologise that I failed to do so and have taken so long to catch up with you. It was the Maharaja's desire that you be presented with this gift upon your return. There are some documents in my briefcase for you to sign which will transfer the deed to your name.

'The deed? You mean he's not just letting me stay here?'

Mr Worthington chuckled. 'No, Mrs Fisher. He is giving you the house. I believe he said that it was too far from London for his purposes. The house and all its contents are yours. You will not even need to furnish unless you tire of the décor.'

He was trying to take me to the house, but I couldn't get my feet to move. How was this my house? How could I even contemplate living here? It was too much, not just as a gift, but for me as a person to manage. 'How am I ever going to manage this place?' I wailed. 'It's too big, I'll never be able to keep it clean.' I wasn't making any sense, I knew that, but my senses were so overloaded that I felt like crying and the house was just too big and too scary.

Mr Worthington came back a few steps to rejoin me. With a soft, kind voice, he said, 'I believe the Maharaja has considered that also. The house comes with live in staff: a gardener, a handy man, a chef and a cleaner. In fact, the only position unfilled was that of butler.' My heart stopped beating, I knew what he was going to say next and I started running. Calling after me, Mr Worthington said, 'The Maharaja was very specific about who I was to offer employment to.'

As I hit the bottom step, the double sized front door opened ahead of me and a tall, dark-skinned figure stepped into the light. He looked at me as I raced toward him and started moving to intercept me, his mouth opening as he said, 'Good afternoon, madam.'

We met on the top step as I leapt into his arms and clung to him. By this point I was bawling my eyes out and unable to speak. Jermaine was here. Jermaine was here and he had accepted the post as my butler in this stupidly grand house and my life would be forevermore complete.

They say you can hug a person for three seconds before it starts becoming weird. Well, Jermaine and I remained rooted to the same spot for more than a minute. Neither of us said anything, not that I could if I tried, but eventually, through the joyful tears, I managed to croak, 'How?'

He pulled away and straightened his jacket, taking a silk handkerchief from a pocket to hand me. As I dabbed my eyes, he said, 'I was approached to take the position a short while ago.'

'How long ago?' I asked suspiciously.

'Two weeks, madam.'

'Two weeks! You've known about this for two weeks!' I slapped his arm as hard as I could, which was much like slapping a lamppost and stung my hand in much the same way.

'I was instructed to keep it a secret, madam. You were to be surprised upon your return to Southampton. Apparently, that did not happen quite as planned.'

Mr Worthington was waiting patiently a short way off. When I turned toward him with a questioning look, he said, 'The deeds, Mrs Fisher. I just need you to sign some paperwork and I will get out of your way. No doubt you would like to explore and meet your staff. I believe the car collection is quite something.'

I felt dizzy again. Car Collection? Staff? 'Hold on,' I begged. 'How am I supposed to pay the staff?' They would all be out of a job in a week. It was one thing to give me a house, but I didn't have the money to pay for it to be run.

Mr Worthington just smiled at me. 'They are all employed by the Maharaja, Mrs Fisher. As will be any new staff you see fit to take on. All maintenance and upkeep of the house is to be paid for by the palace until such time as you choose to sell it. Please believe me when I say that you have nothing to worry about.' Mr Worthington started up the final step toward the front door, but Jermaine stopped him with a quick gesture before turning back to address me. 'There is one more thing I need to share with you, madam. One more unexpected surprise, if you will.'

I wasn't sure I could take another shock; I was still reeling from this one. More than anything, I needed a lie down. 'What is it?' I squeaked in a mix of terror and excitement.

'It's me,' said a blonde voice from the doorway behind Jermaine. Standing in the doorway, and looking as perfect and radiant as ever, was Barbara Berkeley. My legs began to collapse, and Jermaine had to dart forward to catch me.

'How?' I asked, not for the first time.

Barbie joined Jermaine and me on the steps. Since he already had his arms around me to keep me from the floor, she threw her arms around the pair of us, shouting, 'Group hug.' When she released us a few seconds later, she explained, 'Hideki got his junior year assignment. He's going to St Barts in London. I thought you might let me crash here for a few days until I get a place of my own.'

'Are you kidding?' I sobbed. 'I think there's probably a spare bedroom or two here.'

'There are fourteen, madam,' Jermaine supplied.

'Then you are staying with me. Besides, I might need your help.'

'Oh, yes,' she replied, her enormous grin back in place where one could usually find it. 'Jermaine tells me you have opened your own private investigations business.'

I stood staring at the pair of them with an open mouth. 'How the hell do you know that?'

She grinned and nudged Jermaine, who then made a big show of taking out his wallet and being disappointed at having to hand her a crisp twenty pounds note. 'Jermaine and I had a little wager on what you would do next.' Then she stuck out her hand for me to take. 'Come on, Patty, you have to see inside this place. It's enormous.'

I took her hand and then grabbed Jermaine's and like Dorothy and pals going down the yellow brick road, we skipped into the house.

The End

Author Note:

Hello, dear reader,

When I set out to write this series at the start of 2019, I had a very definite plan for what it was going to be, how it was going to go and how it would end. About halfway through the first book I threw all my plans in the trash and wrote from the heart. If you somehow missed the dedication in the very first book, it was the receptionist at the firm in which I used to work who inspired this series. Without her they may never have occurred. Patricia grew in my imagination, becoming a bigger and bigger character until I felt no choice but to set aside the series of paranormal suspense adventures I had been writing to focus instead on her tale. I am so glad I did.

What I hadn't expected as I came into this series, was how the characters would affect me. Writing the growing relationship between Patricia and Jermaine was difficult at times, mostly because it went against the fan mail and emails I kept getting in which fans excitedly looked forward to seeing Patricia and Alistair sail into the sunset together. It was never an option for me; not with where I wanted Patricia's life to go. Alistair may yet return; Patricia just isn't ready for that level of commitment yet and I am writing mystery, not romance. I will admit without shame that I cried at my keyboard when I wrote the last chapter of this book. I'm nearly fifty, I was a soldier for twenty-five years, and I cried when I visualised her being reunited with Jermaine. Then I cried again when I brought Barbie back too. My characters are very much a part of my life. So much so, in fact, that I worry my wife is thoroughly bored of hearing my musings.

Writing ten books plus the short story, *Killer Cocktail*, took me a little more than half a year. As I write this author's note, it is early in the morning on January 3rd 2020, so with the series finished just as the New Year gets underway, what's next? I am currently working on four different series. One is an urban fantasy series with wizards and werewolves and other such wonderous creatures living among us. That may very well not interest you as a fan of Patricia Fisher, but the news that I plan two more series for her should. Patricia Fisher Cruise Mysteries may be finished but Patricia Fisher Village Mysteries will be along soon and another series, as yet untitled, will see Patricia Fisher teaming up with Tempest Michaels from my Blue Moon series when she is hired to investigate a case that's a little spookier than she is used to. That won't be the end of the cozy mystery writing for me though as I already have much more planned.

If you want to know more, or to keep up to date with what I am doing, you can click the link below to get a copy of *Killer Cocktail* and sign up for my newsletter. It's not spam, it's chock-full of fun stuff, bargains, competitions and opportunities. You'll love it, I promise.

Yes! Send me my FREE Patricia Fisher story!

The cruise series has ended but follow me on Amazon for updates of new Patricia Fisher series coming or like me on Facebook to keep up to date with all that is happening.

Website

Facebook

Printed in Great Britain
by Amazon